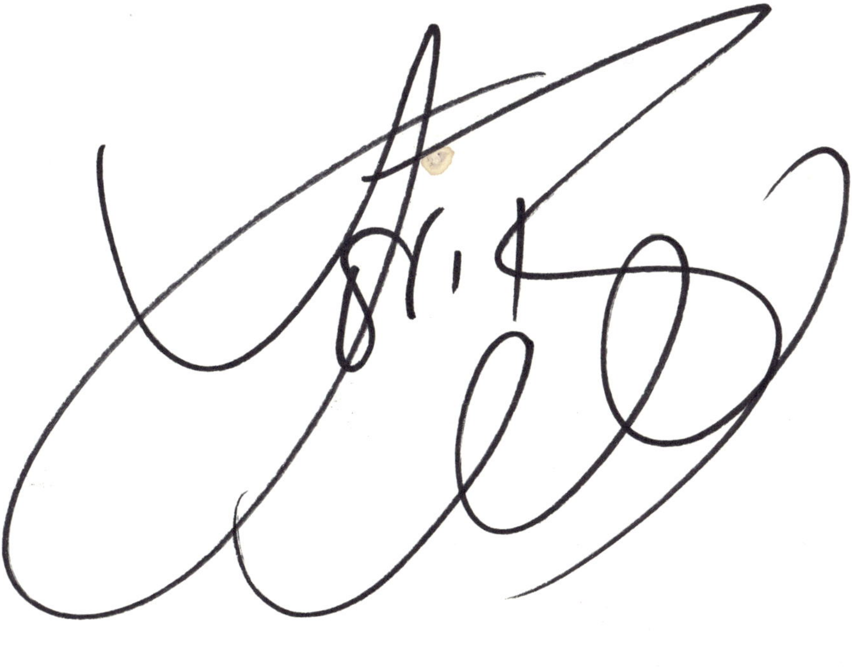

For Reasons Unknown

Book 3

Stronger than Truth Trilogy

Lori Bell

This book is a work of fiction. Names, characters, places and incidents are the product of the author's imagination or are used fictitiously. Any resemblance to actual events, locales, or persons, living or dead, is coincidental.

Copyright © 2019 by Lori Bell

All rights reserved. This book or any portion thereof may not be reproduced or used in any manner whatsoever without the express written permission of the publisher except for the use of brief quotations in a book review.

Cover photograph by CanStock Photo

Printed by CreateSpace

ISBN 978 1699372333

DEDICATION

To being selfless, fierce, and brave.

Chapter 1

Afton Drury held up the back of her hand. She didn't just admire the sizeable diamond ring that caught the early morning sunlight through the window, she felt every ounce of joy from that symbolic promise. Knox Manning completed her life, her entire being, her very soul. The future was theirs.

~

Skye Gallant opened her eyes and had never felt more peaceful when she saw the man lying next to her. Dylan Fruend was her doctor. He was the hematologist-oncologist who had diagnosed her several months ago with myeloma, a rare form of blood cancer. She was considered to be in remission, thus far. She would beg and bargain with a greater power, and absolutely do anything to keep living for her children and now for a man that she already believed would be the love of her life. But the threat of this illness taught her something she never fathomed before. The future was uncertain.

~

Laney Potter packed one suitcase at sunrise. Her husband of more than two decades was afraid to ask where she decided to go. *Was she moving out of their home only because he told her he could no longer live with the ramifications of her drinking problem? Or had she understood his plea and the dire need for her to seek rehabilitation and return to him and their twin sons?* Sobriety was Brad Potters' solution for them to find normalcy again. But, for Laney, that felt entirely too far out of reach.

Laney was in her late forties. She was a grown woman who could take care of herself. But now she only wanted to reach out to her sisters, Afton and Skye. They would know what to say, or do, to help her save her marriage. She couldn't lose the only man she had ever loved. She wished she could make her husband understand. And he expected her to realize the destruction of her dependence on alcohol. The future, their happiness, was in jeopardy.

~

Brad was waiting in the kitchen when Laney made her way from their upstairs bedroom. She carried her suitcase with her and placed it on the floor near the table. There were heavy, uncomfortable emotions between them right now. Since they had fallen in love in high school, they had never been separated. And once they were married, they hadn't spent a single night apart.

This was the first time something had threatened their unbreakable bond.

Laney looked at her husband. He stood with his back against the countertop. He wore a white t-shirt and faded denim, which was his typical construction attire. Laney assumed he was going to work today. No matter where she was supposed to be going, he would resume his normal routine. That seemed unfair to her. He told Laney that she had to get out. She had to choose between admitting herself into an alcohol rehabilitation facility, or just moving out of her own home. *Where would she go? Would she stay with one of her sisters? Would she waste rent money they didn't have on an apartment somewhere in the Twin Cities? And then what?*

"Where are you going?" her husband spoke first. She could see the wavering emotion on his face, and all she wanted to do at the moment was run to him and fall into his arms. He was her safe haven. But this time he wouldn't hold her or make love to her. Brad gave her an ultimatum. To face her drinking addiction, or leave.

"I wish this wasn't happening," she admitted to him. Her voice cracked. "It doesn't have to come to this, Brad. We are stronger than this. We love each other, and being together is all we've ever wanted. That's never changed between us."

"I want that. I do," he began. "I want you here with me, and our boys. I can't stand the thought of going to sleep without you next to me."

Laney smiled. This was her man. The one who could push everything aside and just love her. "Take me upstairs. We'll lock the door. We need to be together."

Brad stopped her from talking. "That will not change the hard truth. You need to drink. You cannot function an entire day or night without putting alcohol in your body. Get some help, Lane. Save yourself from that insanity. Do it for us, and for our family."

She didn't see the error of her ways, or the slow destruction of her addiction. And Brad was unable to fully grasp that Laney's alcohol dependence was a sickness. His wife could not just flip a switch and be better, or simply be able to stop her overwhelming need to drink. "You want me to commit to some sort of program that will force me to abstain from alcohol. And if I don't agree, if I don't check myself into that Eden House in Minneapolis where there already is a room reserved in my name, well then you just want me out of our home." Brad never took his eyes off her. She was dressed in wide-leg black pants, open-toed black heels, and a fitted sleeveless olive-green button-down blouse. This was work attire for her. "I can't just drop everything. I have a career. I have the boys to take care of. I will not abandon either. There are AA meetings and counselors and outpatient treatment. There are other options, Brad."

"What did you decide?" He cut her short. He didn't budge or have an open mind for any other options.

"I want you to hear me out. Compromise, for chrissakes!" She was angry now. Their marriage was a two-way street. It was 50/50. It was give-and-take. He had never made her feel so powerless before, as if her rights didn't matter. He didn't own her, and certainly did not control her. This was *her* life. And her choice.

Before Laney could continue, before she could lash out at him for his unfairness, their 13-year-old son, Luke interrupted.

She read the panic in his eyes when he walked into the room. Laney assumed he was reacting to the suitcase at her feet. "Is Liam here?" he immediately spoke. Liam was his fraternal twin brother, who was older than him by only a minute and a half.

"He's not upstairs?" Laney asked, looking from her son to her husband.

"I don't want to get him in trouble, but I'm worried. He didn't come home last night. His bed hasn't been slept in. I was hoping he just crashed down here on the couch or something." Luke could no longer keep silent in an effort to protect his brother. He had never stayed out all night long before. *Something had to be wrong.*

"What do you mean he didn't come home last night? He was here. He was with you in your room when we all went to bed last night." Laney suddenly lost any sense of calm that she was trying to hold onto.

"He snuck out at midnight to meet Shey. She picked him up to go for a drive or something."

Brad grabbed his cell phone on the counter behind him and spoke as he attempted to call his other son. "What else did he say? Tell us what you know." He pressed his phone to his ear and never took his eyes off Luke.

"That's all. They were going to drive around, probably park, I don't know, get together I guess." Their teenage son made fleeting eye contact with them, as the subject matter was nothing less than incredibly embarrassing.

"This is unbelievable!" Laney interjected, in disgust. "She's sixteen and he's thirteen! This should not be happening."

"Lane," Brad caught her attention. "Let's not worry about that right now. We have to find them. It doesn't sound like his intentions were to stay out all night. And now he's not answering his phone." Brad shoved his phone in the back pocket of his jeans.

"We have to call the police!" she reacted. Just the mere idea of needing the help of law enforcement for anything regarding her children frightened Laney beyond comprehension.

"We're going next door to Shey's parents first."

Luke stood in the kitchen in gym shorts and a t-shirt that looked like it had been slept in. He watched his parents scurry out the door. And then he again looked down at the suitcase on the floor.

~

Dylan Fruend opened his eyes to find the most beautiful woman beside him. "You're real," he smiled, and rubbed the sleep from his eyes. "I wondered if I just had the best dream ever." Skye giggled. She had been lying there, purposely still, just watching him asleep beside her. They made love for the first time last night, all night long. And she knew, for the first time in her life, she was truly in love.

"Last night was as real as it gets," she spoke, moving closer to him, their naked bodies partially covered with only a coral-colored bedsheet. She initiated the kiss. That was just one of the things that Dylan already loved about the woman in his arms. She didn't wait for things to happen. She made them happen.

Later, Skye was stepping out of the shower when she instantly felt lightheaded. She reached for the towel rack and held on. She took a deep breath to stable herself. She was able to wrap a towel around herself, but that nearly overexerted her. She called out his name once, and luckily Dylan had not stepped out of the bedroom yet, as he was already showered, dressed, and ready to go downstairs to see what he could scrounge up for breakfast for them. He moved quick and opened the bathroom door to find Skye standing upright, with one shoulder resting against the wall.

"You okay?" He reached for her. He had her now. "Easy… let's get you to sit down for a moment." He suggested the closed lid of the toilet close by, but Skye insisted she could make it to the foot-end of her bed. He chided himself. He should have known better. They were up almost all night. She needed her rest then, and nourishment this morning. "You should eat something, and your meds are downstairs in the kitchen. Those iron pills are going to keep these episodes from happening." *He hoped.* Dylan looked at her for a long moment. Her color was good. Her breathing was no longer rapid.

She smiled.

"What?" he asked.

"You're giving me that doctor look."

"I am a doctor," he smirked.

"I'm okay now, Dylan. Really. Not much sleep last night," she winked, and touched her fingertips to his lips.

"That's my fault. I need to take better care of you." She had, after all, just been in the ER for a fainting spell. A blood test revealed she was anemic. There was a deficiency of red blood cells, or dysfunctional red blood cells in Skye's body. That condition led to reduced oxygen flow to the body's organs, which explained Skye being lightheaded. Anemia could also be a complication from the myeloma.

"Oh I can't imagine better care than you gave me last night." She giggled and he took her face in his hands as he sat beside her.

"I promise you, Skye. I will take care of you. You're going to be okay." She let him pull her close and hold her. He couldn't make those kinds of promises, she wanted to tell him. But she refrained. Because she wanted to believe him.

~

Afton helped get the girls fed, dressed, and packed into the backseat of Knox's car. He was going to drive them to daycare before he went to Regency Memorial Hospital in Minneapolis, where he had spent the last eight years as an orthopedic surgeon. At the end of the day, the house they were leaving this morning would be quiet again as the girls would return to their mother for a few days.

The baby, Blair, was Knox's biological daughter that he shared with Afton's sister, Skye. The process of in vitro fertilization gave them a miracle. Big sister, Bella was almost four years old now. Knox had not fathered her by blood, but he loved her all the same.

They laughed at the sight of how crammed his car was with car seats, baby gear, and a diaper bag. Just a month ago, Knox and Afton had been living together alone in Saint Paul, Minnesota in that older Victorian style house on Holly Avenue. And now he was a first-time father of two children. Both his heart and his home were full.

"Might be time for a bigger vehicle," Afton winked at him when he was ready to move to the driver's seat.

"But I love my car…" he whined, and she laughed out loud. He moved closer to her and kissed her full on the mouth. "And I love you, my future wife."

She placed both of her palms on his chest. "That sounds nice." She held up her left hand, the one with the flashy diamond on her finger. Afton was engaged to the love of her life. And it had taken her half of her life to find him. It didn't matter that she was in her early fifties and he was seven years younger. They were soul mates. Afton was overjoyed for Knox to be a father, finally living his dream to have a child of his own. She was truly happy to share her life with him.

Knox laced his fingers through her short, cropped pixie haircut. "You have to get moving, or you'll be late," she smiled at him.

He grinned as he got behind the wheel. Gosh he still felt the high of knowing she agreed to marry him last night. Their life had become chaotic while raising babies and juggling a back-and-forth custody schedule with Skye. It wasn't always going to be pure bliss and smooth sailing, but whose life ever was?

Afton stood on the pavement and watched them drive away. It was a different kind of life that she lived now, but those three were her new family. Still, they were her sister's children. She caught herself humming aloud as she turned and walked back into the house. "Que Sera Sera… Whatever will be, will be."

Chapter 2

Even though the Gallant sisters had their own problems and separate lives, they always managed to come together and be there for each other. Skye and Afton met at the main entrance of Regency Memorial Hospital in Minneapolis after Laney had summoned them when *her boy was in trouble.*

~

Code Cliff, on the outskirts of Minneapolis, drew tourists all over the country. The wooded hiking trails, recreational setting, and cliff jumping were the attractions. A view of Code Cliff could be seen from a drive-up spot, overlooking the 80-foot jump. Loitering teenagers parked in their cars had hung out there for generations. Liam and his girlfriend, Shey had chosen that spot to lose their virginity together. It was romantic, she had told him. She was 16 years old. She was a woman compared to the girls his own age. They only had buds, not breasts. They were awkward and inexperienced, not confident. Liam believed her when she told him she had never gone all the way before with any other guy, but she wanted to give herself completely to him. At midnight, they drove to the cliff.

They were the sole car there. Liam followed Shey into the backseat. It was dark. Crammed. Sweaty. Liam fumbled with the condom in the foil packet that he had taken out of his wallet. He practiced this in the dark before. It was awkward at first for both of them as they struggled to find a comfortable feeling in an uncomfortable state. But in no time their raging hormones led them every inch of the way. Inexperienced touches and kisses before it was time to do it. Shey winced and said it felt pinchy. Liam tried not to hurt her. He was overcome with what they were doing though. She never asked him to stop, and he wasn't sure if he could have. But he would have, because he cared about her. He loved her. It was sloppy and awkward and over too soon. But they did it.

They pulled their clothes back on, and Shey wanted to document the location of their first time with a photo. She led Liam to the railing of the cliff. The area was lit, and they could look down and see the cliff, and the Mississippi River that dropped down below. Shey had her cell phone in her hand. "Come closer," she said and had her back against the railing. Liam met her there. He put his arm around her lower back. *She was his girl. He was a man now.* Still coming down from the high of what they had just done in the backseat of a car. Shey held up her phone and was dissatisfied with the angle. "I want more of the cliff drop. The camera flash will catch it if we move a little more." Liam told her they couldn't, and he noted the protective railing directly behind them. She kissed him full and wet on the mouth. He was lost in her. Liam would do anything *his girlfriend* asked. The last words she said to him were, "Let's climb over it…"

It was uncertain if either of them would remember who lost their footing first, standing backwards on uneven, steep rock at the edge of the river. Or if they would survive to tell of the accident.

~

A squad car had pulled up curbside in their neighborhood, just as Laney and Brad were walking through their own yard to get to the neighbor's house. The police officer informed them of the emergency. Two teenagers had fallen off Code Cliff and into the river in the middle of the night. One of them had made a dire attempt to save the other. Both were transported to Regency Memorial.

Laney and Brad found themselves face to face with the emergency room doctor before they could see their son, or learn his fate. Laney was trembling. She wanted to blurt out that *her son has a condition. His lungs are not healthy. The smallest airways of his lungs are damaged, and he coughs and sometimes feels shortness of breath.* But she listened first.

"Your son is alive," were the doctor's first words. The middle-aged man must have been a parent too, because he told Laney and Brad exactly what they needed to hear first and foremost. The details and the specifics of Liam's medical condition would come next. "Liam has a dislocated shoulder, which is minor, considering the dangerous fall he took. But, he's also been placed on a ventilator." Laney brought her hand to her mouth, and no sound escaped. Then she heard Brad react with, "Oh my God," and felt him suddenly take her hand.

"It's just a precautionary measure. Your son can breathe on his own."

"But his lungs…" Laney interrupted, finally able to find her voice.

"His lungs are crippled. Because his airways were already compromised, the water that got into his lungs while he was submerged has intensified his condition. It's a good thing the young lady with him was able to save him. She got ahold of him and kept his head above water and swam herself and him to shore. He was quickly running out of air."

Shey saved his life, Laney's thoughts raced. *Was she supposed to be grateful to the girl who convinced her boy to grow up entirely too fast?* Well, gratitude was the absolute farthest thing from her mind right now.

"Is he going to survive this?" Laney choked out those words. The words that felt foreign on her tongue and made her close her eyes when she heard them with her own ears. *This was her son she was talking about! He could die.*

The doctor responded, "What your son already had before his accident last night was an irreversible lung condition. Parts of his lungs have no air movement or oxygen or carbon dioxide exchange. The ventilator will aide his breathing for awhile. The seriousness of this is he is at risk for having collapsed lungs. The blunt impact to his chest when he fell into the water could have caused air or water to leak into the space between the lungs and the chest wall. We will continue to watch him closely. Mr. and Mrs. Potter, your son is not in the best of shape as of now, but we will do everything possible to save him."

"Thank you," Brad spoke up. He was still tightly holding Laney's hand.

"When can we see him?" was all Laney wanted to know. No more medical terminology or forewarnings of her son not making it through this health crisis.

"Right this way."

~

Brad stepped out into the hallway to call his other son. He told Luke everything. As shocking and painful as it was to hear, it would have been worse to protect him from the truth. Especially if his brother did not pull through. The sight of his 13-year-old son lying in that hospital bed, with machines beeping and pumping oxygen into his lungs, was horrifying. When he escaped the room to call Luke, he then gave in to his pleas to come and get him so he could be with his brother. Brad contemplated how he was going to tell Laney that he had to leave her side for a little while to bring Luke back there with them. And that's when he saw Laney's sisters rushing down the corridor to where he stood.

"What the hell happened?" Skye spoke first.

"Liam snuck out of the house last night to be with his girlfriend." Afton and Skye both knew she was the *older* neighbor girl. "They ended up at Code Cliff, to park, I guess. We don't know anything for sure, and we certainly have no idea how they ended up falling into the river, almost a hundred feet below."

Skye hooked her arm through Afton's. She was her big sister. A decade of life separated them growing up, but as adults they were closer than ever. While Skye was the one presumed to always have it together, Afton actually did.

"How bad is he?" Afton asked, and she and Skye both imagined the lack of oxygen and water in his already fragile lungs.

"Not good," Brad responded, "but could be worse, if you want to look on the positive side. No broken bones, just a dislocated shoulder. He's also on a ventilator, but it's only assisting his lungs for the time being."

Both of Laney's sisters reacted in shock. They had no words at first, until Skye spoke. "So, his lungs are worse now?"

"Sounds that way, but they will heal. Liam is a strong boy. He can fight this." It was difficult to tell if Brad was only grasping onto some sort of hope in an effort to keep himself together.

Brad asked them to stay with Laney while he picked up Luke from home. When he walked away from them, Afton shook her head, and fought the tears welling up in her eyes. "Stop it," Skye scolded her. Laney needs us. No matter how hopeless this looks to us, we do not let her know it."

Afton reached for Skye's hand. "Right." Skye's own life-threatening illness had changed her. She may have become the toughest one of the Gallant sisters. "Let's go to her."

Chapter 3

Laney sat at her son's bedside. She held his hand in both of her own. And she spoke only encouraging words. But she also spoke his language. "Yeah you shouldn't have snuck out of the house to do God knows what with Shey. No, I take that back. I know what teenagers do in the backseat of cars. We can talk about that later. Maybe." She only wanted both her sons to always be safe… and to be smart. She believed she had preached that enough. Evidently, she had not. "Your lungs took a hard hit in that water, Liam. This machine that you're hearing and likely feeling right now will help you to recover quicker." The doctor had explained that Liam was in a medical-induced coma. It was temporary, just until his lungs began to heal. With all of the wires and tubes, it would be too difficult for him to communicate if he were awake, Laney knew. She looked at the breathing tube that was inserted into his mouth and down his airway. Her boy, who so desperately wanted to be a man in charge of himself already, could not have looked more youthful or helpless to her now. She squeezed his hand in hers. "You're going to be okay."

She heard the door to Liam's hospital room close behind her. Laney turned away from her son and she saw her sisters. She placed Liam's hand on the bed, at his side. She stood up, counting on her shaky, unsteady legs to hold her up. Laney should not have been thinking about this right now. But she couldn't help herself. *She needed a drink.*

They were enveloped in a group hug. Muffled sobs were heard among them. Laney eventually regained her composure first. "He's going to pull through this." She was reassuring herself as she spoke those words. Both of her sisters nodded.

"Of course he will," Afton responded, and Skye wondered if giving anyone false hope was the answer in a time of crisis. She would have that conversation with Dylan Fruend. They were no longer just doctor-patient, they were *together*, but she still wanted him to still be completely honest with her, and not to protect her feelings. Or balk at squashing her hope. Skye was confident in facing the facts to enhance her survival. Knowledge was power. Bravery was stronger than truth. She could beat the cancer that currently laid dormant in her body. At the very least, she had to believe that.

Laney shared the facts that she knew about her son's condition thus far. She had the support and love of her sisters, she knew that. She felt that. Both of them were there for her in her desperate time of need. But would either one of them help her get what she needed right now to stay focused on Liam's recovery? And to simply function. Laney's hands were trembling again. And her armpits pooled with perspiration. She wanted a drink to help herself deal with this crisis.

"You okay?" Afton asked her, as they still remained standing close in their half circle near Liam's hospital bed. "Is there anything we can get you, or do for you?" Laney watched both of her sisters make brief eye contact with each other and then back at her. She knew what they were thinking. *They were judging her.*

"I need for my son to be okay. I want my family back together. Brad and both of our boys are my life."

Skye creased her brow. Afton didn't react, but she definitely read more into Laney's desperate words. This wasn't only about her son's health and questionable survival. "Tell us what's going on. All of it," Skye was adamant.

Laney kept her voice low. She believed Liam could hear her every word, especially when she had been at his bedside, pleading with him to stay strong and get well. "Brad thinks my drinking has changed me." She spoke in the simplest, most direct terms. "He said he doesn't like who I've become, or what it's done to our relationship and our family." Once again, Afton and Skye stood in that hospital in stunned silence. They didn't disagree with their brother-in-law. "He sort of kicked me out last night, well, this morning I was supposed to pack a bag and leave."

"What do you mean sort of? And where did he expect you to go?" Afton found herself in protective sister mode. *Yes, she agreed with Brad. But couldn't there have been a gentler, kinder way to reach his wife?*

"He gave me a choice. I could check myself into a 6-week program at the Eden House, it's a rehab facility in the Twin Cities," she clarified, "or just leave. Move out and stay away as long as I needed alcohol."

"That sounds more like an ultimatum," Skye noted. "One, that, either way you lose."

"Exactly!" Laney agreed. She wanted to keep her voice down but had not managed to do so with that reaction.

"No, not exactly," Afton chided both of them. "Your excessive drinking has to stop. Don't move out of your home and away from your entire world of love and support. You will only sink deeper into this hole you're barely able to see out of right now. Get some help, Lane."

"So your vote is the Eden House," Laney appeared miffed at her older sister. "What about you, Skye?"

"Not me. You. What did you decide this morning, or did Liam's emergency hinder all of that?"

It definitely had. The single suitcase that she had packed was still taking up space on her kitchen floor at home. "I packed, but I also got ready for work. I told Brad that I am not going to abandon my sons, nor will I leave my job."

"So, what were you packed for then? Where were you planning to go after the school bell rang this afternoon?" Skye's curiosity had piqued. Both she and Afton did not believe Laney had yet reached the stage where she wanted to help herself. She could admit she craved alcohol, but she didn't see it as a problem.

"I honestly don't know. I packed a few things because Brad was so adamant about it. But I couldn't see myself doing either one of those things. All I wanted to do was convince him that we belong together and that there are other ways for me to seek help, if that's what he wanted." Afton caught Skye's eye. They both understood that it shouldn't be what Brad wanted. It had to be what Laney knew she needed for herself, in order to stop consuming alcohol. "I do think if Luke hadn't interjected with the news that Liam was gone all night long and still missing this morning, we could have worked it out. I tried to remind him that he and I didn't always needs words to communicate."

"Sex isn't the answer to everything," Afton stated, clearly annoyed.

"But it has been a useful distraction for us for as long as we've known each other. But, this time, Brad was just so angry with me…"

"Your focus now should be on Liam. He needs both of his parents, and you need to prove to your husband that you can stay sober." Skye's words made sense, but actually doing that was going to challenge Laney more than ever. She knew that for certain, because all she could think about in her son's hospital room, besides his survival, was how much she needed a drink.

"Right, and it is," Laney spoke, hoping her sisters would believe her. And at that moment she knew that she could not depend on either of them to help her appease that voice in her head preaching that she needed alcohol. *Again and again.* They just didn't understand that she had to drink to function. This crisis with her son had her unraveling.

Chapter 4

Afton drove up the driveway at the home she shared with Knox. She left the car running to rush inside for her camera bag that she left behind this morning in a hurry to meet Skye at the hospital. Afton planned to spend the rest of the day editing at her photography studio downtown Saint Paul. She still had photographs from a recent senior portrait session on her camera that had to be downloaded, so when she realized she left her camera behind, she made a quick trip back home.

She made her way in and out of the house and was walking toward her car when the neighbor lady, probably in her mid to late 70s, called her name. Afton looked, and waved. *She didn't have time for this.* Sandy was standing there in her cotton house dress with a row of white snaps all the way down the front, which ended level with her bare knobby knees.

Afton saw her walking through the yard toward her. *Damn it.* She forced a friendly smile. "How are you today?"

"Achy and miserable in this old body." Afton tried to give her a sympathetic look. She would get older too one day. Afton at least promised herself to never wear a cotton house dress, and to always comb her hair and splash on a little makeup. "This house that Knox bought sat empty for some time," Sandy began to tell what seemed like was going to be a long and unnecessary story. "And then along came Knox...and soon after you shacked up with him." Afton inhaled a slow breath through her nostrils. *Okay fine, that was fair. They were living in sin.* She chuckled to herself. *So be it. If what she and Knox did behind closed doors was sinful, she'll pay the price in the fires of hell. It was worth it.*

"And now, Lord have mercy! There's a baby that's his, but not yours, and there's another child that's neither of yours... and they come and go like foster children! How can you live like that, honey? When I first heard the story about the in vitro and surrogacy, why I didn't believe it! Your sister and your lover? A bit far-fetched to be a reality, isn't it? I mean, who does something like that? Are you an auntie to those children or a step-mother?"

Afton took it all in. She reminded herself that her own mother raised her several decades ago to respect the elders. Neighbor Sandy was making that feat damn near impossible right now. "Sandy, please respect those children in my house, no matter who they belong to biologically. I lived an unhappy and somewhat lonely life before I met Knox," *not that it was any business of hers*, "and now my arms and my heart are full. The circumstances of my niece's birth were anything but far-fetched. She was a preplanned miracle for my family." Sandy stood there in silence for once. The expression on her face was a cross between confusion and irritation, *probably from being called out on her unkind, wrongly assumed words.* "Now, if you'll excuse me… I have to get to work."

~

No matter the fact that she boldly and frankly stood up for herself, the unkind criticism bothered Afton all day long. She was long past the point in her life when she reached the not-giving-a-damn stage. She was at peace with herself, her life, and all of the choices she made. But to be openly judged had gnawed at her relentlessly. This wasn't about her as much as it was about those two little girls. *Would there be a time in their lives when they were bullied or ridiculed?* Afton chided herself for worrying about something so far off into the future that may not ever happen. And if it did, she reminded herself that those children were Gallant girls. Their genes, from a line of strong, resilient women, would see them through the trials and tribulations of life. Afton would instill that in them, as she knew Skye would as well.

Knox was pacing around the empty house after dinner. Afton came from the kitchen and stood in the doorway between the kitchen and the living room and watched him. "You're missing them," she noted.

He stopped and turned to her. He wore a pair of jeans that form fitted his ass and quads. His long-sleeve white oxford was untucked with the sleeves rolled to his elbows. And he was barefoot. Knox Manning was the sexiest human being that Afton had ever laid eyes on. And she had the privilege to lay her hands on him too. She was as grateful now as when they first met that this man desired her too. She was older than him by seven years. Her body was in far less good physical shape than his.

"The house is too quiet when they aren't here. I wish… well you know what I wish."

"For them to live here full-time," Afton stated, and understood, but she wanted to remind him how that was the initial plan all along, going into a life of sharing a child with Skye, and helping to raise Bella as well. Afton was perfectly at ease with how they moved the children back and forth. Truth be told, she enjoyed the time when they could be alone just as much as when they had the girls under their roof. She had her day of raising children. And now she thoroughly loved the perk of being an aunt and a grandmother. *Spoil the little ones and then send them home.* But this was their home, part-time, and Afton was rolling with it. She learned to keep some of those thoughts to herself. Knox wouldn't understand, as he was fully engulfed in being a first-time father.

"I know they can't. I'm just being selfish." Knox sat down on the end of the ivory sectional, and Afton walked into the room and perched her rear on the arm of the furniture near him. She wore a three-quarter-length sleeve denim dress. It raised up and above her knees when she sat down. She tugged at the hem while she spoke.

"You're hardly selfish. You love those girls with everything you have." He palmed her bare knee, and she continued talking. *Why not tell him what was weighing on her mind today? Such petty stuff. But they were partners in this life, and sharing the little things was important too.* "I got caught by our prying neighbor on the driveway this morning."

"Lucky you. What did she want to know now?" Knox had figured out Sandy's type very quickly when he moved into Saint Paul's historic neighborhood.

"It's more like what she already knew. She asked me how I can live like I do… in sin, and raising other people's children. I find her assumptions and her judgment easy to ignore most times, but she criticized the way Blair came into this world as far-fetched and, honestly, I rehashed that all day long. It unnerved me."

Knox shook his head. "She's not worth the wasted negative energy. Far-fetched, though, is something that's unlikely to happen. Skye was going to have a baby through in vitro regardless of who the donor was. The fact that she chose me, so I could be a father was incredible. But what's most important here, is the woman I am madly in love with gave us our blessing. Unlikely to happen? Not if you've ever met a selfless, loyal-to-the-very-end, Gallant girl."

Afton smiled. Knox was right. Sandy had no idea what could be made possible in a world of endless possibilities when there was an abundance of love and respect involved. "You're right. I wasted good energy on someone's else's worthless judgment. I do love our unpredictable life." She leaned down to kiss his lips. He started to unbutton her denim dress from the bottom hem upward. She giggled with her lips still pressed to his. It crossed her mind the way her stomach formed an unattractive roll when she sat down, as Knox seductively peeled away her clothing. She pushed aside her insecurities when she felt his hands on her bare skin. *He loved her. All of her. He wanted her, desired her.*

"Did you say we were accused of living in sin?" Knox teased.

"Uh huh," Afton managed to mumble her answer through his steamy kisses. She was lost in him now.

Her entire dress was unbuttoned. He guided her off the arm of the sectional and down onto his lap. He touched her core through her panties, and moved his hands to her full breasts spilling out of that lacy bra. She reached down to undo the zipper of his denim. And her fingers found him through the gap in those boxer-briefs. He closed his eyes and groaned.

"Let's keep them talking," Knox uttered as more of their clothing was removed and the two of them took full advantage of having an empty house.

Chapter 5

Skye fed Blair a bottle and laid her down in her crib. She watched her nestle in her sleep for a moment. She was already growing and changing at just several weeks old. She looked like a Gallant girl, as Knox liked to say. She already had the caramel brown hairs sprouting from her little round head. Not at all like her big sister when she was born with a full head of thick, dark hair and still had that as a toddler. That little Gallant girl in her crib right now resembled Knox too. Her nose. Her cheekbones. The way her tiny eyebrows arched were like Knox's. She had his full lips and the smile that formed with them. She was a beautiful baby. Skye hoped with every ounce of her being that she would live years, long enough to see her daughters grow into women. *It could happen.* In her sporadic research, and with Dylan's professional knowledge, Skye was aware that some patients with myeloma beat the odds and lived ten to twenty years, or more. And some, overall, lived about three years.

Downstairs, in the living room, Skye found Dylan and Bella, side by side on the sofa. She had her iPad, and he had his laptop. They were both intently glued to their separate screens. Yet this was a bonding moment. Sitting close. Bella's little body was curled into his. They were comfortable together. The connection her little girl shared with Knox was one of a kind. She had not warmed up to her Uncle Brad in the same way she had with Knox. And now there was Dylan. He was respectful of the fact that Bella never had a father in her life, not until Knox had become one to her newborn sister and a father-figure to her. Bella and Knox had a special bond, but it also looked as if she and Dylan were on their way to forming one of their own. They shared silence sometimes and sat close like now, or they often played and took walks together. Dylan Fruend may not even have realized it, but Skye could see him slowly winning her daughter's heart.

Skye watched Bella lose interest in the game on her iPad. She stood up on the sofa and put her little hand on the top of Dylan's hairless head. She rubbed it. He stopped looking at the laptop in front of him and turned to her and grinned. They were eye to eye. "You have no hair," Bella noted.

"That's right, my head is what's called, bald. No hair. Just skin. Bald."

Bella giggled. "Did it fall out?"

"Sort off. Well, most of it did. I don't have good hair, or hair all over my head, so I like to shave it all off."

"I like it," Bella stated, and rubbed both of her palms on the top of his head now.

Dylan laughed out loud, grabbed her gently and squeezed her playfully as he hoisted her into the air above his bald head. She squealed. She giggled. And that's when Skye stepped all the way into the room.

"Shhh… you two are going to wake our sleeping baby upstairs."

"Mommy, Dylan is bald."

Skye muffled a giggle. "I know he is, honey." Dylan winked at her. *Sexy as hell, too*, but Skye kept that observation to herself right now.

"He didn't like his hair, so he shaved it all off," Bella began, on a mission to talk and be heard. "Mommy, when you have a messy hair day, are you going to shave all yours off?" It was an innocent question. How many times hadn't she complained about her long blonde highlighted locks. But this time that particular question was tough to answer. *Would she be so sick one day that she would lose all of her hair?* Dylan watched the emotion change on Skye's face.

"No more talk about hair. I'm hungry. Why don't we go get that snack you wanted earlier?"

Skye watched Bella bounce off the sofa. "You didn't have to protect me like that. I can answer those kinds of questions without falling apart. That could be me one day though. I may get really sick and have to endure treatment that will rob me of my hair." And so much more.

"Hey…" Dylan reached for her hand in the air between sofas. "Having no hair isn't such a bad thing."

"Right," she smiled, "but I'm not into being one of those couples who gradually begins to look alike."

He chuckled. "That's my girl."

When Dylan was summoned into the kitchen by Bella, Skye swatted his ass when he walked past her. She moved to the other sofa then, and picked up the iPad to set it on the coffee table in front of her. She then glanced at the laptop screen. She assumed Dylan was working. She read the headline for the article on the page. *Closer to a Cure for Myeloma.*

Before she read further, Dylan came back into the living room. "Can we interest you in a nutritious snack?"

She looked up from his laptop. "Um, no. Your research here has piqued by curiosity. Are you holding out on me, Fruend?"

"Not at all. As your doctor, I want to learn more than I already know about this disease." He wanted to tell her to pay no mind to that one word… cure. But it had caught his attention too. Sure there were stories out there, success stories, beat-the-odds stories. And he had never paid so close attention to them before now. It was his job to soak up more knowledge about myeloma, and all of it escalated his own hopes of finding a cure. He didn't want Skye to be misled, so he wasn't quite sure how to address this with her right now.

"Does this article say there is a cure?"

"I'm combing through it. I think it's possible, yes, but the answer for you may not be in that particular piece. Stay with me. I've got you. You don't have to read that. I will."

"Stop trying to protect me in that way," Skye was serious. She wanted him to share the pros, the cons, the good, the bad and the ugly with her. She was a big girl. This was, after all, her body that was dealing with something foreign and destructive. But Dylan only wanted to protect her from falling into a hole of doubt and despair.

"I can't," Dylan creased his brow, just as they both heard Bella call out his name again from the kitchen. And then he turned around and walked away.

Skye began to read the information in front of her. *Cure could be too strong of a word to use at this time, but it certainly wasn't out of reach.*

She had a sleeping baby upstairs, and a little girl that she could hear talking nonstop to a man who just might be her own stepdaddy one day. Those were her reasons to inch closer to a cure for a disease that threatened to take away her happiness. Skye read on.

~

Later, when they were alone, Skye approached Dylan again on the subject of this being *her* battle. "I read the article," she said to him, as they lay in bed. No cell phones. No television. Just the two of them between the sheets, talking. "It's promising to think that there could be a cure."

Dylan nodded. "Research leads to successful findings all the time, so yes it's just a matter of time before you are as good as new." He reached for her hand.

"Don't do that," she stated and released herself from his touch. She turned and propped herself up on one elbow to see him. "I am still me. I am the same person you met almost an entire year ago. In your office, you used to tell me everything that was going on inside my body. What changed? Because you are in my bed, do you feel like you must tackle my disease alone like some kind of fucking warrior or something? You love me, I get it. I love you more. Now stop trying to save the day, Fruend!"

He stayed silent for a moment to let her words just wash over him. She was a piece of work. *A woman who could hold her own. Speak her mind. Love fiercely.* "You love me more?" he sidestepped the real issue.

"Don't do that!" Skye reacted. "Stop talking around what I want to discuss with you. I am sick. You are a man, a medical specialist yes, but you are not God. You can't save me if I am not supposed to live."

Then he would die trying. "First of all, I hear you. And I promise not to keep certain research or findings to myself. There are some things that I just don't share with you because so much of this is open-ended. Is it fact? Trial and error? What will be the right fit for you if the myeloma does come out of remission? Those are all things I consider as I research. I am sorry if you are offended because you think I have become possessive of you in some way. It's not like that, Skye."

"It seems like that sometimes, or it at least feels like you are trying to take over without including me," she admitted. "Look, I see you as someone in my future, in the lives of my children. You would not be sleeping over all the time if I did not want you to be a part of our lives." She smiled. He took her hand again and intertwined her fingers with his. And this time she didn't pull away.

"And I want you and your girls in my life forever."

"Then promise me we can go back to talking about the serious stuff. Include me. I won't break."

"I know. You're the toughest woman I've ever met."

"Toughest, huh?" she smiled, and he knew she was past her anger with him.

"Yep," he nodded.

"That's all? Just toughest? Not most beautiful or fit and fabulous?"

"Well… maybe hottest and sexiest…"

"Go on," Skye giggled.

"Gorgeous and definitely the loudest."

She laughed out loud and slapped his t-shirt clad chest. He rolled over on top of her and kissed her lightly and then more aggressively on the lips. "You're the woman I love," he told her. "I will always protect you. I'm sorry that I upset you. Stay on me to be more open with anything you want to talk about."

"I believe you're on me right now," she deadpanned.

"Exactly where I want to be," he kissed her full and hard on the mouth, and she responded. She rolled his t-shirt up and off of his fit torso. She moved her hands down to get him out of those boxer shorts. He was completely naked. So much skin. Head to toe. She ran her hands over his tight chest, down his abs, and lower. He hardened. He knelt over her body. He took ahold of the hem of her satin, spaghetti strapped nightgown, and he slipped it off of her. She was completely naked underneath. He touched her, all of her. He brought his mouth to her breasts, her flat stomach, and down to her core. She muffled her moans. They had little ones asleep just down the hallway. She called out his name, a little louder than she should have. He was driving her to the brink. "Now," she told him, "I can't wait. Just take me, please." Dylan watched her slide out from underneath his body and bend to her knees on top of the bed. He wrapped his arms around her and held her from behind. He touched her breasts, fingered her core. She begged once more. "Dylan, please." He pushed himself inside of her and rocked her body with his. With every thrust, he found himself physically deeper and emotionally more in love with this woman than ever before. Again, he thought to himself... amid unbelievable ecstasy... how he would do absolutely anything possible to save her life.

Chapter 6

Twenty-four hours later, Laney was still at Liam's bedside. Brad had gone home and returned. They both agreed that Luke shouldn't be alone in their home, especially at night. He, too, was reeling from the severity of his brother's condition.

Among feeling so many other emotions, Laney was proud of herself when she opened her eyes the following morning. She survived the night without a drink. There was obviously no place on the hospital grounds to buy alcohol, and she forbade herself to leave her son's side. He and his recovery were most important to her now. And, her marriage that she needed to save. She and Brad were distant but talking for the sake of their son.

When Brad walked back into their son's hospital room, he stared at Laney for a long moment.

"Hi," she said to him.

"Morning. How's Liam?"

"Quiet, and just so still, but I know he can hear me when I talk to him. He understands that he has to rest in order for his lungs to heal."

"Has the doctor said how long that will take? Days? Weeks?"

Laney shook her head.

"Are you okay? Did you get any sleep in that chair?"

"I was able to close my eyes for awhile."

"Did you venture out of this room, for something to eat or—" he stopped himself.

"Drink? I drank a Coke after midnight, Brad. That's all. There's no open bar here."

He attempted to smile. "Right."

"Are we going to talk about it?" Laney confronted her husband.

"Not here. Nothing can happen, no decisions should be made until Liam is safe and sound at home again."

Laney was relieved, but still upset with her son's actions. "Until the next time he does something as careless as vaping or having sex on a cliff! Jesus. Can't you see that this boy's choices have driven me to the brink of insanity?"

"So, you're saying that when we go home, it's back to the bottle if our teenage son doesn't toe the line?" Brad was being snarky, and Laney hardly recognized him.

"No," well damn it, she didn't know that for sure. She hoped not. But needing a drink had been known to out-will her. "All I'm asking is for you to be patient with me. This is all so hard," she turned back to her son lying pretty much lifeless on that bed.

She felt Brad's hand on her shoulder. He stepped closer behind her and stayed there. Laney reached across her chest and held his hand. He didn't say he was sorry for being accusatory and hurtful, and she never swore to stop drinking. This felt like a time-out in their relationship, while they waited for their son to get well.

∼

The doctor made his rounds that morning, after Liam had been taken away for additional tests. He had something new to tell Brad and Laney this time. "We need to remove the ventilator," were his first words. Laney wanted to interrupt and ask why, because she thought it was helping his lungs to heal. That's what they were told, that's what she had been telling herself for hours on end as she watched her son in that dreadful, helpless state. "A common risk of being on a machine like this is to develop ventilator-associated pneumonia. The tube that was placed in his airway can allow bacteria to enter the lungs."

"That quickly?" Brad interjected. "You're telling us that being on this machine yesterday and last night gave our son pneumonia?"

"It's unclear," the doctor explained. "There's also the fact that he has water in his lungs from the cliff fall. We too must consider the e-juice that has been pooling in his lungs and possibly filling up just as fluid causing pneumonia would."

"But what if my son hasn't vaped in months?" Laney questioned Liam's honesty, but defended him.

"That may not even matter," the doctor stated as fact. "So now we immediately remove the vent and begin to treat him for pneumonia. Please understand that this is going to be a long, risky road. Damaged lungs do not handle infection well. I will be upfront with you both," the doctor paused, "your son's condition is now life-threatening."

~

Laney struggled to catch her own breath. The ventilator would be removed from Liam's airway. The medication for his induced comatose state would also cease. He was one sick boy. He could fight the pneumonia though. He had to. Brad stood with her right outside of the doorway of Liam's hospital room. "Do you want do go grab something from the cafeteria? You need to eat to keep up your own strength."

"Thanks, but I'm not hungry."

"Eat anyway, Lane. Come on. Walk with me." His arm around the small of her back almost made her worries fade away. She needed him by her side more than she ever realized. And she knew they would physically be apart right now if it had not been for Liam's health crisis. It felt strange to be grateful for timing of that, but she needed to feel something other than afraid for her son's life. If he did survive this, would his quality of life be hindered because he had the lungs equivalent to an old man? *One worry at a time*, Laney told herself. And she focused on her husband by her side.

Chapter 7

Jess Robertson wore her highest navy heels. A long, fitted navy dress with cap sleeves and a moderate slit on the side of one leg formed her sleek figure. She had just concluded handling a funeral all afternoon. She led the family as they said their final goodbyes at the funeral home, then attended a memorial ceremony at the church, and finally gathered for the burial at the cemetery. This was what her colleagues would describe as a standard funeral. The woman lived to be 89 years old. She had a full, wonderful life with six children and seventeen grandchildren and equally as many great grandchildren. But Jess still found it to be terribly sad. Letting go was extremely difficult, whether it was someone who had a long, well-lived life, or someone like her own husband, Mark who died unexpectedly of a heart attack two years ago. She still grieved for him. She may not have been the perfect wife, but she had loved him. Jess was certain her late husband would be proud of her now. She had officially completed mortuary school and had taken over as the mortician and director of his family-owned Robertson Funeral Home in Saint Paul. Mark's cousin, Patrick spearheaded the same business in Minneapolis. He had taken Jess under his wing for her apprenticeship as she earned her degree. Patrick, at 45 years old, was a decade younger than Jess. He had a wife and three young children. But that had not stopped him from crossing the line a few times with Jess. She tried to fend off his flirty words and unsubtle advances. She had been down that road before. She wouldn't have an affair with a married man again. Her best friend, Afton hadn't stopped reminding her of the risks. Jess knew better. Even still, she had slept with Patrick.

She was alone in the funeral home, putting everything back in order from the events earlier in the day. She heard the security system alert. Everyone on staff had a key to the back door. A few minutes later, Patrick stood across the funeral parlor from her. He wore a black suit, a solid charcoal gray tie, and shiny black shoes. He was tall, broad shouldered. His dark hair was always styled with product. Jess knew that it didn't feel soft when she ran her fingers through it during sex with him.

"How'd it go today?" he asked her.

"Very well. No glitches."

"You look beautiful in that dress," he noted. Her long legs were endless in those high heels. Patrick wanted to feel them wrapped around his bare back again.

"Thank you," she accepted the compliment. "What brings you by?" This was her place now. She was no longer under his wing. She just assumed this was a business call. She secretly hoped since they no longer worked side-by-side, that maybe their intimacy would cease. The temptation for her was undeniable when he was around. She contemplated explaining that to him, if she had to. They needed to stop their affair.

"Not business, if that's what you're wondering. I was hoping we could grab a drink?"

"Patrick, not in public. You know how that will look." The times they had gotten together were under that very roof. It was safe. No one could know. Jess had managed to keep a decade-long affair with Sam Drury private until his wife (who was now her best friend, Afton) eventually found out. Her friendship with Afton was thriving now, but Sam's life had ended. It was self-defense. He was going to strangle his wife to death in order to pursue a life with Jess, but it was Jess who saved Afton from her own husband. One strike over the head with a fireplace poker and Sam Drury was dead. She only meant to stop him, not kill him. Jess and Afton covered up his death in the crematory of Robertson Funeral Home. He remained a missing person in the Twin Cities.

"Hear me out, please. I am so close to hiring a lawyer. I want a divorce. You know that has been a long time coming. Being with you now though has opened my eyes to what we could have. You and I could be a powerhouse together, owning and running both businesses. I want you by my side like that, Jess."

Jess stood there, listening but not wanting any part of being a team with him. She worked hard for where she was now, at the helm. She didn't want to share the spotlight or a life with Patrick. Her solid, respectable image would be tarnished if the community discovered she was the other woman who broke up a marriage and a family. "I can't take that risk. Go home to your family. Focus on rebuilding that part of your life, Patrick." Jess paused. This was going to be more difficult that she initially believed. "What we've done should not have happened. I'm lonely, and I'm just so vulnerable with you. I'm not saying you took advantage of that. It's me, as well. But it was sex, Patrick. Physical need. It can't happen again."

They stood together in the middle of the empty parlor. It was quiet in there. Not eerie. Not to them. They were used to the surroundings. An empty metal rack that supported a coffin just hours ago. A bare pedestal where a guestbook was placed. Sporadic flower pedals on the floor. Empty rows of chairs. Her narrow heels dug into the carpet as she stood toe to toe with Patrick.

"I know you're afraid of what could happen," he stated, and that could not have been farther from the truth. Jess had her thoughts and emotions together. She didn't fear people finding out, because she wasn't going to take that risk. Not any farther than she already had with her late husband's younger cousin. "People get over gossip. Time passes. For me, you are worth it if I'm scorned for awhile."

"I'm not making this public with you. And I won't be the reason you leave your wife. It's over, Patrick."

"Okay, okay," he threw up his hands in the space between them. "I am moving too fast. Let's just be together. You said it was just sex. But I know I've made love to you. You're lonely. Let me take care of those needs." Jess chided herself for feeling weak in the knees right now. She switched her weight from both legs to one, and then back to both. "I want you, Jess. I want to touch you. Let's go to your office. No strings. Forget my overreaction. This is on your terms. I promise. Women usually want commitment. You're not like most woman. I understand that now. I just got a little caught up in you and this," he said, and he touched his open palm to her arm, just above the elbow. She couldn't deny that she missed a man's touch. She was very attracted to him. She could have sex, and then just carry on again. At the end of every single day, her big house was too quiet and when she lay in her bed alone, her body ached to be touched. At fifty-five years old, she still had a remarkable sex-drive. She touched his hand on her arm. He watched her expression change. She had gone from adamant to stop this, to having that wanting look in her eyes. Patrick was a proud, arrogant man. He had a way with women, and this one was no exception. He bent his head down to kiss her. Lightly. She whimpered. More aggressively. She met his tongue with hers. She pulled away quickly.

"Not here."

He walked behind her to her office. He watched the way her bottom swayed in that fitted dress.

She slammed the door to her office when he followed her inside. She was upset with herself for letting this happen. But she damned those feelings. She needed to be wanted by a man. So, Patrick it was.

He pressed her against the door. She stepped out of the dress that he unzipped, and it was quickly at her ankles. He tore off his own shirt. She undid and pulled off his belt. His pants were undone. Her bra lacy stayed on. Her thong was half off when they dropped to the floor against the door. He asked her to do things to him each time they had sex. She enjoyed the turn on when he told her what he liked. She now did the same. Their passion was explosive as they were attentive to each other, and eager. Yet again, Jess Robertson had lost control with a man who desired her beyond all rationality. And, as she had known all too well, there were ramifications to a man's obsession.

~

As Jess was about to step up and into her black Escalade on the grounds of the funeral home, Afton drove up.

She parked her car alongside of Jess, let it run idle, and rolled down her window. "I saw you about to leave as I was driving by. On your way home already?" Afton knew that sometimes Jess worked much later than a typical quitting time.

Their separate lives and busy work schedules kept them from staying in close touch lately.

"I am, but no one awaits, so no hurry," Jess noted, and Afton turned off her engine and stepped out her car. Jess pulled her into a tight hug and she secretly hoped she didn't reek of sex. As with the other two times she was with Patrick, she now felt remorseful afterward. "Tell me what's on your mind," Jess spoke as they parted. She hoped Afton's nephew's condition was improving.

"Honestly, I miss you — and I'm checking up on you. Can't I do that from time to time?" Afton asked her, and Jess felt uneasy as if she could read her mind. Afton knew the temptation Jess fought when it came to Patrick Robertson. But that was all Afton had known. Jess hadn't told her that she succumbed to sex with him. And she didn't want to tell her. Now, or ever. But, she would. Keeping secrets from each other was a thing of their past.

"I'm consumed with work, which I like," Jess smiled.

"Good. Does Patrick come around since you took over this place as your own?" And there it was. The topic Jess didn't want to come up.

"Occasionally, yes. We do run both businesses together, in a sense." Afton watched her body language. She bit her bottom lip mid-sentence. She made fleeting eye contact as if to be distracted by cars driving by. She ran her fingers through her long, dark hair twice.

"There's something you're not telling me. You did it, didn't you? You slept with him." Their friendship was once one of shared small talk and empty compliments. This newfound trust and love between them mirrored a sisterhood pact to always be straightforward and truthful with each other. Even if it crossed boundaries. Or pissed each other off.

"Is that why you're here? That's why you veered off the beaten path tonight? You saw me and wanted to accuse me of doing the one thing I've told you that I have been fighting myself not to do?"

"I'm sorry," Afton told her. "That was insensitive of me. I wanted to see you. I'm just worried about you is all, and you're acting jumpy or uninterested in talking to me right now. I just assumed. And I was wrong to do that."

"You're not wrong," Jess confessed. "I'm in too deep again. I have no self-control when it comes to a man I'm attracted to. It's happened. I've been with him a few times."

Afton looked away from Jess for a moment. She allowed this to wash over her. She needed to respond, not react. "So, you're telling yourself it's just sex? I know you, Jess. And I know it's enough for you to meet those desires and carry on. What about him though? You're screwing a married man again. I don't have to tell you where that will lead."

"I've made myself very clear. It's sex only."

"But?"

"But he wants to leave his wife for me."

"Jesus, Jess! He has little kids."

"I know that. And I won't be a part of that destruction."

"But you already are! Don't you see? Patrick has fallen for you, as any man with eyes and a responsive dick would!" Afton never shied away from telling her best friend she was an ageless, beautiful woman.

"I told him today that I wanted to stop this, and just end it."

"And?"

"As you said, I have no self-control. We did it against the door in my office."

Afton frowned. "Thanks for the visual."

"I'm ashamed, I really am."

"But you can't stop yourself."

"Aft… have you ever laid in bed alone while the loneliness just crept over your body? I don't want Patrick Robertson as my life partner, but I do want someone to talk to, to love me, and need me. I wish to share my life with someone again. Because I don't have that kind of intimacy, I want what I can get at the moment. Physical intimacy. It's a temporary high, I know that. But for right now, it's enough."

Afton couldn't argue with her, or judge her. "Just be careful. Give him your body then, but not your soul."

Jess had tears in her eyes when Afton reached out to her and they held each other just outside Robertson Funeral Home. "You smell like sex," Afton noted, as she spoke aloud in her ear. And they both giggled.

Chapter 8

"You should be the one to go home and stay with Luke tonight," Brad offered, as he and Laney sat together at Liam's bedside. It was late, and both Afton and Skye had just left when visiting hours were over.

Laney looked at him before she answered. She didn't trust herself outside of that hospital room. She was under a dry roof now. There was alcohol in their house. Even in places Brad had no idea she had stashed it for emergencies, which were the times she ran out of it.

"I want to be here when he wakes up," she stated.

"The doctor said it could be 12 to 72 hours. I promise I'll call you if he stirs." For hours the only noise, now that the tubes and wires attached to machines had been removed from him, were his breathing that sounded more like wheezing at times, and occasional coughing. It was strange to watch him cough without ever opening his eyes.

"Brad," she spoke softly. "I don't trust myself." She didn't have to elaborate. He understood what she meant. He watched her eyes well up with tears, and she could no longer look at him. He moved closer to her.

"That's good. You're telling me how you feel. You're admitting a weakness and acknowledging out loud that you are safe from temptation inside these walls."

"No, that's not good. I want a drink, Brad. And if I'm at home, I know I can get one."

"I got rid of it all. I threw it out. It's okay, Lane." But he didn't know there was more that she had hidden. He was too trusting of her. Or naïve to an addict's ways. *Was that what she was?* Laney stayed silent. "I'm proud of you. Keep fighting this. I know you are strong enough to beat this, and to stay sober."

Laney smiled at him, but that smile never met her eyes. "I still don't know if I can leave him." She glanced at their son, still so lifeless on the bed.

"Luke needs you, too. He's been asking a lot of questions that I can't answer the way that you can. I don't want to tell him that his brother is going to be okay when you and I still don't know that for certain. I can't lie to him, so I only told him it's bad. I think I made things worse. He cried, Lane. He needs his mom right now. Just go. I'll stay."

"Will you hold me?" she asked him, and he opened his arms to her. She needed to feel loved and trusted in his arms. She would freeze that moment and the feeling in her mind for later when she was tempted to take a drink. She didn't want to disappoint him.

~

Laney walked into her home. Luke was due any moment to be dropped off from football practice. All she wanted to do was take a long, hot shower, and fall into bed. But Brad wouldn't be there beside her. And Liam wouldn't in the bedroom down the hallway that he shared with his twin brother. They all needed to be together. This wasn't right. Terrible things were threatening to separate her family.

She thought of the bottle of vodka that she had stashed in the basement in a cardboard box marked, Christmas decorations. And then there was the wine, a bottle on its side, under the sink in the master bathroom behind a few boxes of tampons. Laney closed her eyes and then shut them tighter. "No," she spoke aloud, standing in the middle of the living room where she hadn't turned a single light on yet.

"Mom?"

She jumped. "Luke," she reached for the nearest lamp, "you startled me!"

"I'm sorry. Why were you talking to yourself?"

"I wasn't," she defended her sanity. "Fine, I was. Never mind. I'm just worried about your brother and my thoughts are racing. I guess one of those words just got out of my head." It was a dumb reason for talking to herself, but Luke smiled regardless.

"Dad said you're staying here tonight. What if Liam wakes up?"

"Your dad is with him if he does. I know you need me, too," Laney spoke as she stepped toward her son. Luke was the good boy. His grades were high scores. Sports were his passion. And he always wanted to please his parents. Laney reached for him and opened her arms, and he fell into them. He cried. Laney cried. And finally, Luke wiped the tears off his face and spoke.

"What's going to happen if Liam dies, mom?"

"Don't think like that," she couldn't fathom her world without her two sons and Brad. "He's not going to." Luke believed his mother.

"Then what about you and Dad? Are you still going to live here with us when Liam comes home from the hospital?"

Laney's eyes were wide. He knew something. It was that damn suitcase, still on the kitchen floor. It sat there like a lone missing puzzle piece. If she moved out, their family would forever be incomplete. "I'm not going anywhere, Luke," was all she offered as an explanation.

"Stop treating me like a little kid. You don't brush off Liam like that. You make him talk about the serious shit."

"Watch your mouth," Laney gave him the stern, I-will-beat-your-butt look that only a mother could master.

"Sorry, but I mean it, mom. I heard you and Dad talking. He wanted you to leave."

"No, he doesn't really want me to leave. He loves me. He just wants me to—"

"Stop drinking." Her son finished her sentence for her. But there was something about the way he said those words that sounded as if he was telling her to do the same. *To please just stop drinking.*

She didn't know how to explain it to her son. She couldn't even simplify this for herself. Yes, she drank. But she had just gone nearly 36 hours without drinking any alcohol. If she could function without it, that wasn't addiction. She was, however, thinking about it. Almost constantly. And that was a problem.

"Your dad and I are not going to separate," she reassured her son. "I promise, I will do whatever it takes to keep our family together. And that includes helping your brother get well again."

Luke nodded, but he didn't like the way his mother never addressed her drinking problem. She hadn't even denied having one.

~

Laney stepped out of the shower. She wrapped a towel around her head to soak the water dripping off her hair. She took a second towel and tightened it around her torso. She stood in front of the vanity. The mirror was completely steamed over from that long-awaited hot shower she needed. She bent to her knees and opened the cabinet door below the sink. She reached behind the tampon boxes and found that bottle of wine on its side. It rolled away from her, farther back into the dark cabinet, and so she reached again to grasp it. She held that bottle by the neck, as she stood up. The steam from the mirror was beginning to lift. The movement on the floor had caused the towel to slip off her head. It fell to her shoulder and then onto the floor. She could see her reflection in the mirror now. Her hair had sporadic grays, especially around her ears. The whites of her eyes were red from lack of sleep. Her makeup-free face looked a little pale. The freckles across the bridge of her nose were highly visible. She didn't like to look at herself for long periods of time in the mirror anymore. Not like when she was younger. She still had a pretty good body. But her face showed age. Crow's feet. Laugh Lines.

Forehead wrinkles. She saw the stress of her life staring back at her. Her son's shenanigans had aged her in recent years. That, she knew for certain. And the wine bottle in her hand was what she turned to when she needed an uplift. Oddly, that solution to hoist her above her problems was now her downfall.

The bottle in her hand angered her. She was a self-sufficient, independent woman. Why hadn't she known better? She hated knowing her son had damaged his body by vaping. What she was doing was really no different. Liam even tried to tell her that. She was hurting herself. She watched the tears roll down her cheeks. The reflection staring back at her was of a woman who had lost control. And at this helpless, hopeless moment, she felt too far gone to care.

Laney's hand trembled as she twisted off the cap from the wine bottle. The rim of it was warm to her lips. She tipped it into her mouth. One swallow tasted bitter. She didn't welcome it. It wasn't the long-awaited wave of relief she had anticipated. Rather, she felt ashamed. Locked behind her bathroom door. Naked underneath a draped towel, with raw emotions consuming her mind. She held the bottle over the sink, and she began to pour and empty all of it. The drain couldn't keep up as the white wine pooled and bubbled. She could smell it. She dropped the empty bottle into the bowl of the sink now and backed away. She tugged at the damp towel around her body and fastened it tighter with one hand. She unlocked her bathroom door, turned off the light, and made her way over to her and Brad's empty bed. She laid on top of the duvet on Brad's side. And she cried into his pillow.

What felt like a victory for her at this defining moment had also brought her to her knees. *What if the next time she wasn't able to drain that bottle anywhere else but into her own body?*

Chapter 9

Restful sleep never came for Laney the night before. She got up early and put herself together to return to the hospital once she drove Luke to school. She had taken a week off from teaching, with hope that Liam would begin to show improvement.

When Laney was driving alone, about three miles from Regency Memorial, she received a text from Brad.

He's awake!

She didn't reply. She only pressed her foot down harder on the gas pedal. She needed to get to her boy as soon as she possibly could.

She practically sprinted through the lobby and down the hospital corridors. When she pushed open the door, she saw Liam sitting up in bed — while their teenage neighbor girl was seated on the chair beside him. Laney immediately stopped. The smile on her face began to fade. *Was she supposed to say something out of gratitude to this girl? Shey had, after all, saved her son from drowning. But, yet, she was the reason her son was at Code Cliff in the middle of the night.* Laney quickly regained her composure. She was the adult here. Her son was awake — and alive for heaven's sake — and now was not the time to judge or ridicule anyone. She would, however, address how she felt to her son when they were alone later.

"Well hi there... look at you." Liam attempted to respond to her, but he broke into a cough instead. A long, lingering hack that made Laney's eyes water. He pressed on his chest when the cough subsided. "You okay? How bad does it hurt?"

"Bad," he groaned.

Laney glanced from her son to Shey, but did not acknowledge her. "You have pneumonia... and a dislocated shoulder," she pointed to the sling around his left shoulder which supported his arm.

"Both are things that will heal with time, that's what Shey told me," Liam noted, and Laney tried to form a smile. *So now the hot little neighbor girl was playing nursemaid to her son as well.*

"She's right," Laney said through her clinched teeth. "Where's your dad?" *Where the hell was Brad? And why was this young girl hanging by her son's bedside as if she was the little wife or something?*

"He went to see about getting me some breakfast. I'm starving."

Laney nodded. "Good. Eat and build up your strength so we can get you out of here. Your brother is beyond worried about you. We all have been."

"I know, and I'm sorry," Liam spoke, with an obvious glance in Shey's direction. "We were at the cliff and we shouldn't have been. It was too dark. We were taking selfies, and we got too close to the edge. We fell over the cliff. I remember when I hit the water, my body hurt so bad. I couldn't find the strength to swim. I went under. Shey saved me, mom. She saved my life."

Oh dear God. Laney thought of how impossible it must have been in the dark of night to see anything in the water. It was a miracle that her son had not drowned. Laney took a few steps closer to Liam on the bed — and near Shey beside it. "Thank you," she paused and looked at Shey. She didn't reach out her hand to touch her or open her arms to hug her. "Liam's dad and I are so grateful for what you did."

"You're welcome," was all she said, which was for the best because Laney was still mad as hell at that 16-year-old cougar. *Liam, three years younger, was barely a teenager for chrissakes!*

"Have you gone back to school yet?" Laney asked her.

"No, but I plan to after my doctor's appointment today."

How insensitive of Laney. Had Shey gotten hurt too when she fell into the river after that 80-foot drop?

"Were you hurt from the fall?"

"No, just a little bruised. My mom insisted that I get checked out."

"You can stop by after school again," Liam chimed in, obviously hopeful that she would come back to see him.

Shey smiled. It was time for her to leave, and Laney was clearly the only one in the room who was on board with that. She watched that young girl, dressed in straw wedges, a short denim skirt, and a very low V-neck white t-shirt. She stood up, moved closer to the bedside, and planted a kiss right on her son's lips. Laney's jaw dropped, right before she rolled her eyes. Liam was a lovestruck puppy with this girl. He was in way over his head with raging hormones and feelings that were far from being hopelessly in love.

"Snap out of it, William Bradley," Laney ordered him when the door closed, and they were finally alone.

"You're mad. It's written all over your face. You don't like Shey anymore, do you?"

"Those are both loaded questions," Laney spoke, and it was her turn to sit down on the bedside chair. "I am very upset with you for sneaking out to do something so dangerous. What were you thinking? Don't answer that. Just know that when you get out of here, I am not waiting around for your dad to have a serious sex talk with you. You and I are going to discuss exactly what you need to be doing to protect yourself since you are going to defy me and do it anyway."

Liam looked down at his lap.

"You already did it, didn't you? You had sex with her on that cliff."

"Woah, let's not go there. Not here, not now, Lane." Brad overheard her when he walked into the room carrying a tray that was heaping with bacon and eggs and toast.

"Nice timing, Brad," Laney chided him, and he shrugged his shoulders. *She would ask her husband later why Shey had shown up just minutes after Liam was awake? Had Brad given him permission or arranged that for him?* Being a father and being a buddy to his teenage son was becoming a blurred line.

Chapter 10

"Dr. Fruend, Skye Gallant is here for her appointment. She's waiting in Room 4." Before the nurse interrupted Dylan, he was lost in research. He had momentarily forgotten that Skye had an appointment today to learn the results of her latest blood draw. And yes, they could have done this at home — her house or his — but they were still doing this the professional way. The only thing Dylan had not done yet, that he said he would eventually do, was to find another specialist for Skye. He wasn't ready to give her up as a patient and just oversee someone else medically taking charge of Skye's condition. What if she agreed with another doctor over him? Dylan chided himself. He was being ridiculous. Even still, Skye was his main concern now, professionally and personally.

He tapped on the door twice before walking in. It's what he did with all of his patients. She smiled when he closed the door behind him.

"Tell me this isn't weird," she spoke first, because that's just what Skye always did.

He chuckled and sat down on the stool in front of her dangled legs on the exam table. "You wore a short skirt today on purpose, didn't you?" he shook his head at her and willed himself not to run his hands over the length of them.

"I have no idea what you're talking about," she laughed out loud, and he watched her for a long moment. She looked healthy and happy. He just had to keep her that way. "You're staring at me," Skye noted.

"I am."

"Just tell me about my test results. I don't know why you couldn't just call me this morning when you read them." She would not have wanted to wait all day for him to tell her tonight at dinner at his house, because Knox had the girls, but they could talk like this anytime now.

"I want your money for the office visit," he teased her.

Skye winked at him, "I have insurance."

"Your levels look good," he got down to the reason she was there. "Iron is still somewhat low, so I will increase the dosage of your pills. I know I ask you this every day, and every night when you're in my arms," she giggled, "but have there been any changes in how you feel? Anything at all?"

"Other than tired because the man I love will not keep his hands off me at bedtime, yeah, I'm okay."

Dylan shook his head. "Liar. You get plenty of sleep. But just to be sure, I'll prescribe sex only in the afternoon from now on."

Skye laughed entirely too loud for being in a small exam room with thin walls and Dylan playfully shushed her.

"We do need to talk about something while I'm here," Skye began, and he listened attentively. "How much longer are you going to be my doctor now that you and I are, well, you know, involved?"

"For as long as I possibly can," he stated. "I'm not in a hurry for that to change." Skye noticed the seriousness on his face.

Good. She didn't want another doctor anyway. "I just thought you could get into trouble if people start talking."

"I'll worry about that. Right now, it's just you and me."

"I like it that way."

Dylan had reached out to Dr. Wesley Wright, a research specialist and professor of cell biology at Saint Louis University. He wasn't a hematologist-oncologist like Dylan, but he did have a remarkable success story to tell as a multiple myeloma survivor. That's right, *a survivor*. Dylan obviously knew they were out there. People who beat all the odds. And he unrealistically wanted to meet them, one by one, to hear their stories. But when he found Dr. Wright's story published in an online medical journal, he immediately knew this was the man to seek out and gain as much insight as possible.

His doctors had fought the disease vigorously for ten years. But after a decade of treatment, Dr. Wright began to run out of options and contemplated looking into hospice. Instead, Wright took a chance and enrolled in a clinical trial to use a living drug that was made by extracting some of his own immune cells, adding genetic code so they would recognize his myeloma and reintroduce the weaponized cells to his body to attack the cancer. Myeloma was thought to be incurable, but four years later Wright now showed no evidence of the disease. He considered himself cured.

Dylan realized he was jumping ahead. Skye had yet to come out of the remission that she remarkably began this diagnosis with several months ago. But if anything were to change, if the cancer became active and aggressive, Dylan wanted to have a plan of action in place. And this was the first time, as a physician, that he considered veering off the beaten path. The thought of Skye enduring years of chemotherapy treatments that may not even be effective had empowered Dylan to research further. And, by chance, he found what he believed could save Skye's life — the same live drug that saved Dr. Wright. Dylan was not going to stop until he talked to that man. Even if it meant traveling to St. Louis to get his attention.

After extensive research, Dylan learned the chimeric antigen receptor (CAR) T-cell therapies, which was the treatment Wright had, was developed for use in other blood cancers and approved by the Food and Drug Administration for certain types of leukemia and lymphoma. He was not going into this blind and careless. This appeared to be a safe and successful method, proven to sustain a complete response — and successfully cure multiple myeloma. But there were roadblocks.

This groundbreaking treatment was offered only in clinical trials and primarily to those patients whose disease had relapsed after many therapies. It also was still inconclusive whether this treatment could be used in cases where patients were in the early stages of the disease. That was Skye's case. And Dylan chose to overlook the fact that researchers were several years away from implementing this regimen on newly diagnosed cancer patients. That, he didn't want to accept. Or, perhaps, Skye had several years of good health ahead of her. He certainly hoped so with all of his heart. But his medical instincts demanded that he be prepared for anything to change at any time. While Skye was still in the calm seas of this disease, Dylan was prepared to work rigorously to learn more about this proven cure, what the drawbacks were, and how Skye could become an accepted candidate for it. That's where he would come into the equation. He would use his status as a renowned hematologist-oncologist in the Twin Cities to get Skye on the patient list for this regimen.

"Your mind is reeling," Skye noticed. "What are you so focused on behind that laptop?" He was like that often times after hours, too.

"Research. It's complicated right now to explain, but I'm learning new ways to help my patients live with what we assume are incurable diseases."

Skye didn't trust anyone else more. She relished in the good news today and had done so each time she learned the cancer in her blood was still in remission. She had prepared herself, however, for the day to come eventually when the news would no longer be good. And that's when she would implement all of her trust in one man. Because she now believed deep in her soul — if Dylan Fruend couldn't save her life, then she wasn't meant to have more time.

She hadn't revealed that to him. Just as Dylan did not share his latest findings with her. Neither one of them wanted to go there. Not yet. Not if they didn't have to. Because it was inevitable that, one day, Dylan would be under tremendous pressure to save Skye's life. And Skye would take a gamble of hope with him. She would risk it, even if it was only false hope. That's the only choice there was with life or death.

Chapter 11

It clearly wasn't unusual for the funeral home to receive deliveries from the local florist. It was, however, odd that there wasn't an upcoming memorial until two days from now, and there was only one vase of a dozen, long-stemmed red roses.

"For you," the delivery boy told Jess once she let him inside the foyer.

"Me? Not just for here, but for me?" She took the roses from him.

"There's a card attached," he noted, and turned to leave before Jess could speak again, or even offer him a monetary tip. She, of course, never tipped the driver after a bulk delivery from one business to another. That would be unnecessary. *But this time the flowers were for her?*

Jess carefully placed the crystal vase on top of the desk in her office. She tore into the small envelop. There wasn't a single woman on earth who didn't feel just a little tickled to get flowers.

Her excitement ceased, however, when she read the handwritten words on the card.

Wait. Don't be upset with me. I know what red roses mean. I could have sent yellow — for warm feelings, joy, and friendship. Or orange — for desire and excitement. But red is what you deserve. Just let me love you…

Patrick

Jess' eyes were wide. She read his note on the card twice. Clever. Touching. But entirely inappropriate. Love? She was far from being in love with Patrick Robertson. They needed a floral color that meant sex. Just sex.

She tore up the card into a lot of little pieces before she threw it in the trash. No good would come from anyone seeing that.

∼

By the week's end, Liam was still very sick, but improving. His body was slowly responding to the antibiotics. His chest hurt to breathe. He began having high fevers with shaking chills, followed by excessive sweating. He was constantly fatigued, but could rarely rest with his persistent cough. Laney had been staying with him at the hospital daily and every night since the one she spent at home. She hadn't had a drink in five days, with the exception of the wine in her bathroom that she took one swallow of before pouring it down the drain. Laney was trying very hard to help herself through this. Oddly, she had been walking the hospital corridors often, and had come across a pamphlet in a waiting room that she now kept tucked inside of her handbag. There were facts and information about detoxing from alcohol. She took that as a sign to get started.

She already had mastered the first step — there was no trace of alcohol in her body anymore. She had flushed all of it out. And she had endured the withdrawal symptoms. The worst for her was the insomnia and the headaches. But being by Liam's side in the hospital had honestly been a good distraction for her. Laney wanted nothing more than for him to get well and to be able to go home and resume his life, but she feared what would happen to her then. *Would she relapse?*

She stepped out into the hallway with her handbag on her shoulder. She was going to go to the cafeteria for something to eat while Liam slept. Whenever he dozed off, she used that time to get some fresh air or to fuel her body with food.

As the door to Liam's hospital room closed behind her, Laney turned to find Afton there. "Hi, are you escaping?" Afton asked, because she noticed her handbag.

"That's definitely what it feels like. I'm going to the cafeteria. Do you want to join me for coffee or something?"

"You drink coffee now?" Afton creased her brow.

"I do. Don't judge. I've replaced alcohol with caffeine."

Afton looked at her sister as they walked side by side. Laney was taller and lankier. Afton was shorter with more muscular limbs. "Judge you? More like, I'm proud of you."

Laney smiled and glanced down at the floor as they walked. "I'm detoxing. It's hard. I can't sleep. I constantly have a headache. But I know it's going to take time for my body to adjust."

Once they found a corner table, Laney dove her fork into a vegetable omelet and drank black coffee, while Afton ate a piece of carrot cake and sipped a bottle of water.

"I'm glad you're here," Laney told her sister.

"I've been worried about you. I thought you would be smuggling vodka in here."

"Don't think I haven't thought about, or done it before," Laney muffled a laugh with her napkin while she had food in her mouth.

"You're doing this to save your marriage," Afton noted. "Is Brad aware?"

Laney nodded. "Besides the fact that we spend all of our time in this hospital to be near our son, he and I are close again. He's relieved. He knows I haven't given in to temptation." Laney chose to keep the wine incident in her bathroom to herself. No one needed to know that she had to hit her lowest point before she began to save herself. "I don't think he realizes though how difficult this is for me. He thinks it's a matter of choice to drink or don't drink. I know that alcohol was a depressant for me. I relied on it over the course of time. I became dependent on having a drink to ease my stress, unwind, or to just enjoy it out of sheer habit."

"It's wonderful that you recognize that," Afton credited her. "Keep it up. I can't imagine it being easy at times."

"At times? Try 24/7," Laney attempted to explain. "I want a drink every minute of the day."

"What happens when you have access to that again? Liam is going to get well and be discharged from this place. What then?"

"It'll get harder," Laney admitted.

"I don't know how you feel or anything close to what you are going through, but I'm here to listen and support you anytime."

Laney shook her head as if she was refusing her offer.

"What? I am."

"Not that. I was just thinking how we have all been through, or are going through, something. You just never know how your life will go."

"Like Skye. What if her cancer becomes aggressive?"

"I'm thinking of all three of us. You've been through crazy with Sam. God only knows where he is! And the whole in vitro thing, which was your idea I'll remind you again. It can't be easy for you to watch Knox raise a baby with Skye."

Afton took in her words. Yes, she was miserable with Sam. She was unhappy for most of her marriage. And now, he was gone. And God wasn't the only one who knew where he was. Sam was her past, and Knox was the man she wanted to share her future with.

"Among all the craziness, we are happy together," Afton finally spoke. "I didn't know a man, a partner in life, like Knox, existed for me. He's an adoring father to both of the girls, and that is another reason why I fall more in love with him all the time."

Laney smiled. "*Both* of the girls. Just like that, he's a father of two."

"He always has loved Bella as his own, so it just made sense to make her and the baby a package deal with the custody arrangement."

"Do you ever wonder who her biological father is? I mean, we know it's someone that Skye was physically with, not a donor. We've suspected that she planned the pregnancy and handpicked the father of her child. It's just something that I've thought about now that Skye is sick. What if, one day, Bella has questions… and her mother isn't here to provide the answers?" It was painful to imagine Skye gone from their lives.

"That's a heavy thought."

"It could happen."

"What are you saying? That we should have an intervention with Skye and get this guy's name and number for Bella's future? She has Knox, and the way things are going she has a pretty remarkable father figure in Dylan Fruend, too."

"I am not denying any of that. I guess I've been in this hospital too long, but I now see this as a medical history thing too for Bella's sake."

"That makes sense, it really does. You can be the one to bring it up to Skye though." Afton laughed, but she seriously meant those words. She would not push this issue. Because she knew all too well what it was like to keep a secret that was better left untold.

Chapter 12

"Did you get the roses?"

That was the unanswered text in Jess' phone messages for two days. Patrick had to know that whatever was going on between the two of them was not going to lead to a relationship. And certainly not love. He fulfilled, okay more like satisfied beyond words, her sexual desires. *Was she still lonely? Yes. But physically her needs were being met.* It was enough for her, but clearly had not been for Patrick.

This affair, however, had to stop. They both had taken things too far. For Jess, sleeping with a married man again was a repetitive pattern that she lived once before, and knew firsthand how deceit could end badly. For Patrick, he wanted more than what Jess did. He believed what they shared was a lasting, leave-your-wife-and-kids kind of love.

Jess made her way home. The estate she shared with her late husband was on the outskirts of Saint Paul, in the countryside. She had a five-thousand-square-foot home on twenty-two acres. When Mark died, she immediately wanted to sell their home. But she was never fully ready to let go yet. Her Escalade rolled over the curb and onto the driveway. She stopped before she opened one of the triple garage doors. She shifted into park quickly, killed the engine, and got out. Her heels hit the concrete hard. She made her way up to the wrap-around front porch, where she had two high-back rocking chairs that were painted cherry red. Sitting back on one was Patrick.

"What the hell are you doing here?" She didn't have neighbors nearby, thank goodness. She could speak loudly out there and not be overheard. But it was time that Patrick heard her.

"You ignored my text," he spoke without taking his eyes off her.

"People are busy, Patrick. Don't get your feelings hurt over the petty stuff. How did you get here? Where is your car?" She glanced out at the street again.

"In the garage. I didn't want to be noticed out here."

"The garage was locked, and so was my house. What the hell, Patrick? Did you break in?" This was a dangerous game she played. First with Sam Drury. And now with Patrick.

"I can assure you no damage was done."

"You need to leave!"

"Roses, Jess. A dozen red roses. Did you read the card attached? I know it seems too soon, but I'm in love with you. I loved you long before you ever let me touch you. Just take this leap with me. We are so good together now… just imagine how much better we'll be."

"It's sex. I thought you understood what we were doing. I'm not in this for love."

She watched his face fall. This often arrogant, over-confident man had been let down. He stood up from the rocking chair. He scuffled his shiny black shoes on the concrete as he stood primarily in place. "Let's go inside. I will convince you otherwise."

Jess thought of the decade-long affair she had with Sam Drury. They were in sync for so long. Forbidden sex was their haven. Until Sam wanted more. Her husband died and Sam believed he owned her. That same uneasy feeling had overcome Jess' conscious right now. The last time she allowed her lover into her home, he ended up dead. Patrick and Sam were alike in many ways, especially when it came down to being men who always got what they wanted. *And they had both wanted her.*

"Get your car out of my garage and go home to your wife." Her voice was calm, but firm, and she never looked away. She stood nearly eye level with him in her heels. "We are over."

"My wife... she's not like you," Patrick began, and appeared to have ignored everything Jess said. "She's so caught up in the kids that she barely sees me. She has lost confidence in herself as a woman. Not too many women carry themselves like you do. You're sexy and self-assured. You are a powerhouse in business, and you take that control to the bedroom. I know what I want in a woman. It's you."

Jess stood there. Silent. She processed all that he had spoken to her before she responded in no uncertain terms. "Your wife is a decade or more younger than I am. She's in an entirely different phase of her life. I've raised my children. The part of my life where I put them first is over. Be more understanding of what her role is right now and do things to make her see that she is beautiful and desired — and more than just a mother to your children. She deserves to be appreciated and paid attention to. Give her that, Patrick."

"What about what I need? I need you." He reached for her. And Jess immediately took two steps backward. All that she had said to him had gone unheard. Just like when she had tried to fight Sam Drury's demands and ultimatums at the end of their affair. Her words had been drowned out by obsession.

"Go. You've taken this too far. Yes, I gave in and I allowed things to happen between us. But I don't want any part of what you are caught up in wanting with me. All I want now is out. No sex. No contact. If we have business to discuss, I want a phone call, not a personal visit. Jess turned her back and walked away from him. She made it to her vehicle and used the remote inside to open the last of the three garage doors. She knew that was the only vacant one for Patrick to park inside. She still wondered how he had gotten inside, but she didn't ask him because the thought of him breaking and entering her home frightened her. And she wouldn't allow him to see her fear. She only wanted him gone now.

Patrick followed her off the porch and stood near her vehicle with her. "You've done this before, haven't you?"

Jess creased her brow and waited for him to clarify his remark.

"Were you faithful to my cousin? Did Mark have your complete loyalty all throughout your marriage to him? Or did you cheat on him? And when you allowed another man put his hands on you, his body joined with yours... did you stomp all over his heart too?" Jess ceased eye contact with him. *What more was there to say? He couldn't possibly know anything about Sam Drury.* "I'll go," Patrick finally obliged, and she had to keep herself from exhaling an obvious sigh of relief. "But I can't live without you. I won't..." his words trailed off as he solemnly turned on his heels in front of her. She never took her eyes off him until he backed out of her garage, off her property, and was out of sight and long gone down the road from her home. That's when Jess was finally able to breathe again.

Chapter 13

Behind closed —and locked— doors, Jess quickly found her phone. She didn't think that Patrick would come back, but if he did, he would find a way inside. He already had once when she was not there.

"Pick up the damn phone!" Jess demanded just as Afton answered on the fourth ring. Jess spoke immediately. "He was here. In my house. He broke in when I was at work. It was so strange. He was waiting for me on my porch and he had his car parked inside my garage!"

"Slow down! Who was?" It had been awhile since Afton heard that kind of panic in Jess' voice. It definitely took her back to those unsettling days with her husband, Sam.

"Patrick. He wants more from me. I told him from the beginning that we were sleeping together and that was all. Physical fun only."

"He clearly has weak comprehension skills," Afton partly joked, and even let out a slight giggle.

"It's not funny. It's like he's obsessed… like Sam was with me… you know, at the end."

Afton momentarily paused. *How could Jess have gotten involved with another married man again? Hadn't she learned a damn thing the first time?* "Where is he now?"

"I sent him away. He drove off. I don't know. I hope he went home."

"But now you're worried that he'll come back?" Afton immediately wanted to go to her. If Patrick did return, Afton had no doubt that Jess could protect herself. She just fretted about that outcome if Patrick was indeed as obsessed with her as she claimed. Jess was a smart woman, but sometimes she needed to be shoved in the direction of better judgment.

Afton stood in her kitchen now. Knox was on his way home with the girls. It was the first of three nights under their roof again, and Afton knew that Knox would need her help. But her best friend needed her more. She told Jess not to leave. She would be right there. And, as Afton went out the door, she texted Knox. He would have to parent on his own for little while tonight.

∼

It took Afton longer to get to Jess than she planned. There was an accident en route to the back roads that led to the Robertson estate. She came to a stop behind a line of traffic. Up ahead, she could see emergency vehicles. She was about to pick up her phone to notify Jess when she recognized a long-time firefighter for Saint Paul walking ahead. He was a friend of Sam's. Chad Willmann walked from car to car. Afton promptly rolled down her window when he reached her. He had a kind face and an infectious smile. And a gift for gab.

His intent was to inform Afton that there would be a significant delay before traffic could pass the scene ahead. But when he saw that it was Afton in the car, he greeted her and never hesitated to answer her when she asked what happened. A lone car had crashed into a utility pole. The driver had not been wearing his seatbelt. He was killed instantly. Afton's response had been to say, "how awful," and that's when Chad Willmann noted *that the Twin Cities had lost another prominent citizen. The community was now sure to mourn the loss of another Robertson.* Patrick Robertson was killed in that car accident merely feet from Afton.

"A one car accident?" Afton asked to clarify what happened. She had to repeat this story to Jess. This was going to be horrifying for her.

"Right. He lost control, we assume. His speed was excessive for this road."

Afton thought it, but never spoke it. *Had Patrick Robertson intentionally gone without the protection of a seat belt and crashed his car into a pole? Did he take his own life once he fled Jess' home?*

~

When Afton finally arrived at Jess' house, she was waiting for her at the door. "I didn't think you were coming after all." Afton hadn't picked up her phone in the car. She didn't have the words then. But she had to pull herself together and speak to her now. Jess took a closer look at Afton once she stepped into the foyer. "Did something happen on your way here?"

Afton nodded. "There was an accident. That's why I'm late."

"You should have turned around. I would have understood."

"I wanted to see you," Afton felt shaky. "I think you need to hear something from me."

Jess' eyes widened. "I don't like the sound of that…"

"The accident was a one-car. It hit a utility pole. The driver lost control, or something, and was killed on impact."

"Oh my gosh. No seatbelt?"

Afton shook her head. "I was told he lost his life instantly. I mean, that's minimal suffering I guess, if anything good has to come of something so tragic. I mean, how do you find peace in something like that at all when it happens to someone close to you?"

"Right," Jess was confused by Afton's rambling. "Afton, did you know the victim?"

"Met him once," she was careful to reply. "Jess… it was Patrick. He died after he left your house."

Jess took a few steps backwards until she was against the wall in that foyer. She pressed her hands behind her, palms flat against the wall. She attempted to hold herself up after hearing the most shocking, unexpected words. "He's gone?"

Afton nodded.

"This can't be true."

"I'm sorry, Jess."

"But it's not my loss. He had a wife and children and a business to run. My God, this is Mark all over again — leaving behind everything and everyone to pick up the pieces." Jess paused for a long while, and Afton moved to be near her. She too pressed her back against the wall beside her. "He was angry when he left here. This was my fault."

"No. I'm not going to let you do that," Afton pushed her body away from the wall and stood in front of Jess. She forced her to look at her. "Patrick was in control of his own damn car."

"And his own damn life..." Jess added in barely a whisper.

"What does that mean?"

"The last thing he said to me after I told him we were over was, 'I'll go, but I can't live without you. I won't.' Patrick was not the kind of man who left things up to fate. He did things in order to stay in control. That car accident was purposeful. He took his own life because of me."

"You can't be sure of that," Afton tried to talk her down from this theory that would only cause her more pain... or guilt.

"No, I can't. But I am."

Afton reached for both of her hands in her own. She grasped them tightly. Her face was now very close to Jess'. "Listen. There is nothing you could have done to prevent this, if this was actually what you are calling it."

"It was suicide. And like hell I couldn't have prevented it. I pushed him away. I told him we were done, and to go home to his wife and children."

"How is that wrong? How can you place yourself at fault for that? He didn't belong with you."

"No. But he needed me. And I failed. I caused a man to end his life. There's a pattern here, don't you see? I cheated on Mark. Then things spiraled out of control with Sam. And now Patrick."

"You did not fail anyone!" Afton was adamant. "Patrick had a mind of his own. He was a grown man with responsibilities and commitments and he's the one who failed if he truly did this to himself. Remember that. Listen to me and listen well. You are a beautiful, self-assured, accomplished woman who captivates attractive, controlling men who end up confusing lust and power with love. How is that your fault when those kinds of men come along and you're attracted to them because of what they can do in the bedroom? What it comes down to is they cannot control their own emotions!"

After Jess allowed that truth to resonate with her, she spoke. "If it's not my fault, then what do I do to stop this cycle from repeating itself again?"

"For starters, stay away from married men!" Afton was halfheartedly teasing just to break up all the tension and the pain of this shock that Jess reeled from right now.

Jess attempted to smile. But it didn't last. She would try very hard not to fault herself for this tragedy. But she feared that preventing anyone else from pointing the blame at her would be impossible — if Patrick Robertson had left behind any trace of his intimacy with her.

Chapter 14

It was 1 a.m. before Afton left Jess. They sat on her sofa in the dark and shared a bottle of wine and tears for a man gone too soon. Jess hadn't loved him, but that didn't matter anymore. The way his story ended would forever sadden her.

While they were sitting close and talking with their voices low because they were emotionally and physically worn out, Jess brought up a subject they hadn't discussed in quite awhile.

"I don't know what I would do without you," she told Afton.

"Oh stop, it's just the alcohol talking," Afton teased.

"No, really. It was your ability to forgive me that saved our friendship. I was not deserving. I've made such a mess of my life and others at times. Sometimes I really think I'm not worthy of genuinely being loved."

"I think the right man just hasn't come along. Sure, you loved Mark, he was the father of your children and you made a great life with him — but you know he wasn't truly the one for you. Sam was an affair, solely for sex, and so was Patrick. You need a Knox in your life. Believe me, I had no idea what I was missing. We have a solid relationship. I want that for you."

And through her tears, Jess had said, "I want that for me too. More than anyone knows." Afton thought about that as she drove back home. Knox was her life now, and she had never been happier.

She stepped through the front door in the dark, into the living room. There was a dim lamp lit near the sectional, and that was just enough to light her path. The house was in disarray with toys and blankets. Afton was blatantly reminded that Knox had the girls alone tonight. She stepped over things on the floor and made her way upstairs. When she entered her bedroom, she found Knox asleep on top of the bedding. And he was still wearing his dress pants, sans a shirt — and on his chest, was his sleeping baby. She stared for a moment. Something was off, as Knox hadn't laid her down in her crib. He opened his eyes now, and put his finger to his lips as if to shush her and she had not even said anything. She watched him lay the baby down on their bed very slowly and cautiously as if not to wake her. Knox then made his way over to her and whispered, "You're finally home."

"Jess needed me," was all she offered, because she didn't want to wake the baby.

"Blair had a fever all night. Bella is battling a cold, and I now think Blair is getting it too."

"Oh no. Rough night," Afton sympathized but had not been overly sympathetic because with kids and babies there were always germs and sickness. She had lived through those times already.

Knox was instantly miffed by her lack of compassion. He turned and walked across the room and into the master bathroom. Afton followed him. She sensed he was overwhelmed tonight, and she wanted to tell him that he would get used the stress of having sick kids. "It will get easier," she said, and he partly closed the door because he now had turned on the bathroom light.

"What will?"

"Dealing with sick little ones. It does get overwhelming."

"I could have used your help, that's all," he snapped at her.

"Knox, you know that Patrick was killed in a car accident, and Jess was distraught. I had to stay with her until I was sure she was okay."

"Right. I just don't like how she's trouble, that's all."

"Trouble?" Afton was offended for her best friend. "She's a grown woman who has made some bad choices. But she's not trouble."

"She had an affair with your husband, while pretending to be your friend. And now she was fending off a younger married man who apparently she gave in to. If she's not trouble, then she's definitely guilty of attracting it!"

"What does that even matter to you?"

"She's a bad influence."

"On me? Really, Knox? I'm not an impressionable teenager."

"I just think you need to scale back on your time spent with her. People who make bad decisions sometimes reel in those closest to them." This was almost comical to Afton. They certainly had gotten themselves into quite a situation that could have led to serious trouble had they not made a genius joint decision regarding Sam's dead body. It was a dire move. And a risky one. *To hell with all that though!*

"Why are we doing this now? I'm tired, and you obviously are too."

"I am. You're right. But before we try to sleep for a few hours, I want to mention I need your help with Blair tomorrow if she still has a fever and cannot go to daycare."

Afton was caught off guard for a moment. "My help? I can't. I have a 9 a.m. shoot."

"Damn it. I have surgeries scheduled all day."

"What about Skye?" *She is her mother,* Afton refrained from saying so.

"She's giving a presentation on web design downtown Minneapolis at one of the convention centers."

"Oh my. We better hope that fever stays away, so Blair can go to daycare."

Knox sat down on the closed toilet lid. He was bare-chested and his dress pants were wrinkled. Poor guy. He did look like he had been through crazy, not even having a second to himself to shower or shed his pants. "She's been crying all night. I held her so she would sleep. The house is a mess because I pretty much allowed Bella to do whatever. But she's coughing and snotty too."

"Welcome to fatherhood," she smiled at him. It certainly wasn't all fun and games.

"Right," he said, running his hands through his disheveled wavy brown hair.

"Are we going to bed?" Afton wanted to get some sleep. It was almost 2 a.m. already.

"I don't want to move her," he referred to his baby. "I think I should stay close, and probably lay with her again." Knox and Afton shared a queen-size bed, and he had just implied that there wasn't enough space for her if a tiny baby was in that bed with him. Or maybe it was a safety factor.

"Oh okay... I can take the sofa." Afton didn't want to go downstairs to sleep on the sectional, but at this point she did just want to get some rest somewhere.

"Thanks," he said, standing up and walking toward the door where she stood. He never kissed her or touched her as he moved past her. And then Afton heard him say, "We can talk again about how we are going to work out staying home with Blair first thing tomorrow."

What? Afton was sure he had just implied that involved her. "Wait," she spoke up, and he turned his body back to her from the doorway, "I told you staying home was not an option for me tomorrow. I mean, I would help if I could, but I cannot cancel a shoot."

For Reasons Unknown

Knox frowned, and then rephrased what they both already knew. "I have a surgery day. And I know Skye cannot get out of her commitment to present." This unnerved Afton, as if he and Skye had both discussed that neither of them could take care of their child, so Afton would likely just drop everything to stay home with their baby. *No one had asked her first!*

"And you think that leaves me to help?" The tone of Afton's voice was louder now, and she knew she needed to quiet down before she woke the baby. "Knox, come on, really? Whose responsibility are those girls? Skye's! And yours! Not mine!" She was tired, and now she was upset. Knox was both as well. In fact, it was his initial snarky attitude the moment she came home in the middle of the night that had sparked her overall resistance.

The look on his face was anger and disappointment. Afton read that very clearly. *But damn it, she was angry too.* She may have gone too far with her words, but the fact of the matter was Knox and Skye were parenting those girls. *Not her.*

As if her timing was perfect, before more words were said that they would regret, Blair began to cry. Knox moved through the doorway without looking back at Afton. She knew this argument was not over, but he had to tend to his baby. Afton stood in their bedroom and watched him attempt to soothe her. She wanted to ask him if he needed a cool washcloth or something, or another dose of Tylenol or Motrin to keep Blair's temperature down. But she was too angry right now. She wouldn't try to help or take responsibility for *his* baby. Afton left the room to go downstairs and attempt to sleep on the sofa — also in the clothes she had worn all day long.

Chapter 15

Afton woke up to a knock on the door. She was startled when she realized where she had fallen asleep. She opened her eyes on the sectional in the living room and heard Knox coming down the stairs. He had the baby in his arms and Bella was trailing behind. When he opened the front door, Afton sat up abruptly.

She had no warning from him if he was expecting someone. This was her house too. She was not presentable. Messy hair. Makeup stained faced. Morning breath. And worst of all, yesterday's shift dress — sans the bra she had taken off and draped over the back of the sofa before she finally fell sleep. She grabbed the bra and wadded it between her two hands as she saw Dylan Fruend walk into her house. Sure, he had been there before. But not unannounced. Afton cursed Knox in her mind right now. *Damn him!*

She watched Knox step back and allow Dylan to come inside. She saw them shake hands, and then heard Knox mention that he would bring Bella to daycare and all Dylan had to do was watch Blair... *the bottles were in the fridge, changing stuff was in the nursery upstairs.*

"Got it. I've been thoroughly briefed by Skye," they both chuckled. They discussed how Skye was going to leave the convention following her presentation and just skip the opportunity to have lunch and network afterward. In the midst of their chatter, Afton stood up. Bella noticed and ran to her, declaring that she was awake.

"Knox said not to wake you," Bella stated, receiving a tight hug from her aunt.

"I gathered that," Afton replied and glared at Knox. She folded her arms across her chest and attempted to tuck her bra underneath her armpit.

Dylan smiled at her.

"Hi Dylan, sorry for the mess and my surprise that you are here. I am going to go upstairs and get ready for work." Again, she glared at Knox. She never asked if Blair still had a fever, because given Dylan's presence there she assumed as much.

This was the first time ever that neither of them said goodbye at the start of their workday. The shared silence between them weighed heavily on Afton. This was not who they were together. And while she believed some of the fault was hers, Knox was also to blame.

Once she showered and got fully dressed upstairs, Afton made her way downstairs again. She needed coffee badly. The start of her day was already awful, she couldn't omit caffeine from it too.

She found Dylan sitting on a quilt on the floor with the baby. He had her lying on her back and she was playing with a soft rattle in both of her hands. The living room had been picked up a little.

"Is this awkward for you?" she asked him, as she made her way down to the floor to finally pay attention to Blair.

"Probably more so for you because I've invaded your space," Dylan noted. "I rescheduled a few of my appointments this morning so I could help out. Skye thought it would be best if I came over here to avoid having to move Blair again."

Great... a renowned medical specialist with an appointment book crammed full of ill patients came to the rescue. Now this photographer looked even worse in everyone else's eyes.

"Thank you for helping," was all she said. She pressed her lips to the baby's forehead, which felt warm.

"It's a stubborn fever, but she'll be fine," Dylan had read her mind and then eased it.

"Good. I need coffee and then I have to go."

"Knox said he made some."

Afton stood up from the floor as she asked Dylan, "Do you drink coffee?"

"No, it's all yours."

Knox didn't drink coffee either. Among the chaotic morning, he had taken the time to make her coffee. And he had let her sleep as well. My goodness, Afton felt like a useless woman this morning.

~

Her nerves were a wreck. Last night, Patrick Robertson's body was removed from the scene of the accident and brought to the Robertson Funeral Home in Minneapolis. Ironically, Patrick's body now laid in the morgue of his own funeral home. His father, who was retired from the same business and handed the legacy down to his son, had brought his body there. And then in the early hours of the morning, he called Jess and asked her if she would take over and get Patrick's body ready and help him handle the funeral at that facility. She was, after all, now a mortician and this was in her job description. No one had any idea though just how difficult it would be for her.

She walked into that funeral home. She was met by Patrick's father. He was an older, distinguished version of Patrick. His eyes were red from crying. And he lost his composure again when Jess offered her sympathy. "He would want you to get him ready." *Why? Did his father know something more?*

"I cared about him. This is such a loss for your family, his wife, his kids, and this community." It felt like losing Mark all over again when the City of Saint Paul mourned a great man that she called her husband. And now it was the City of Minneapolis that was going through the same.

Jess was left alone in that building. She made her way downstairs. His body was the only *customer* at the moment. A sheet was draped entirely over him on a steel table in the middle of the morgue. The sound of Jess' heels on the concrete floor echoed all around her. Her hands were trembling as she peeled back the white sheet from his forehead. She removed it completely and it fell to the floor. He was still dressed in the clothing she had seen him wear last. Dark suit pants, white shirt, red tie, and those shiny black shoes. His face and hands were scraped and bloody in parts. She touched his face. Stone cold and stiff. This wasn't the first time she had seen or touched a dead body. But this was Patrick. A man so full of life… and passion. She closed her eyes to shut out the intimate memories of him. He didn't deserve this.

Jess began to remove his clothing. All of it. She forced herself to be in work mode now. Stripping and then bathing the lifeless body were the first order of business once it was delivered to the morgue of the funeral home. Patrick's father had told her of his wishes upon death. He wanted to be viewed. He knew his family would need that kind of closure. He also wanted to be buried as opposed to cremated. He believed in having a plot in the cemetery, a place marked in the ground for his body one day. Cremation had never appealed to him. His own mother had wished to be burned to ashes, and it always pained him knowing he never had even a shell of her body to bid farewell. He was fifteen years old when he lost her. Jess stared at Patrick's body. Not like a mortician. Not the way she typically would have. This was a man who had taken her own body with his, and that's what she was thinking of now. The sexual desire. The passion. The lust. How he made her feel then would never be again. But that's what she had wanted. She told him so. But the very last thing Jess ever would have wished for was this. *Death. The end of his story.* Patrick should not be dead.

For Reasons Unknown

She bathed his body until the blood stains were gone. The cuts and scrapes and bruises remained. She would attempt to touch up those with makeup.

As Jess prepared to embalm a body, any such body, she always felt like sort of a cross between an artist and a scientist. She appreciated that every human body was a work of art by God. She was fascinated by it. The scientist part of this job was the technique used to preserve the deceased by replacing a portion of their blood with chemicals. Those chemicals are formaldehyde-based solutions. She injected the solution into the body's arteries. This would then reach his body tissue and organs and drain the fluids to slow the decomposition and restore the physical appearance of the body for cosmetic purposes. The living needed to see their loved one, one final time, as they remembered them. Looking as close to lifelike as possible.

Hours later, she applied makeup to his face and neck. When she touched his lips, her vision was clouded by the tears welling up in her eyes. He looked so much like himself still. Jess lathered a generous dab of hair product in both of her hands and she ran her fingers through Patrick's dark, wavy locks one last time. She dabbed away her free-falling tears with the back of her hand. Patrick smelled the same, despite how the scent of embalming fluid had consumed the air down in the basement. Finally, she partially covered his prepared body with a lone, clean white sheet again. She was told by Patrick's father that someone would be sent over with a suit for Patrick to wear in the casket.

Jess had no idea that the delivery person would be Patrick's wife.

She was stunned to see her in the foyer of the funeral home. This place, the building, was not Jess' space, nor was it Patrick's wife's. They were standing in his territory, and it felt incredibly awkward for both of them for entirely different reasons.

Jess had never met her before, nor did she know her name. "I'm Jess Robertson," she began, and was about to offer her condolences.

"I know who you are," the petite redhead spoke. Jess, in heels, towered her. Patrick's wife was hardly a wallflower. Her shoulder-length red hair was striking. Her complexion was like porcelain. She was probably a size eight or ten, and she was curvy in all the right places. She was attractive. Jess was taken aback. She could see her and Patrick as a striking couple. She imagined they made beautiful children together. *Why hadn't Patrick ravished this woman, his wife — and left her well enough alone?* "You took over at Saint Paul's funeral home when Mark died." *Had this woman been to Mark's funeral?* Jess had no recollection. She assumed she had been though because Mark and Patrick were family. *How had Jess not remembered her?* "Patrick spoke highly of you," she added. Jess had to control her reaction to those words.

"I'm so sorry — for you and for your children," Jess spoke sincerely. She watched Patrick's wife (she didn't even know her first name) get teary-eyed.

"Thank you. It's awful for them. It's my children who will mourn him forever. My pain is for them." That was a somewhat strange way to put it, Jess thought, but she understood. She, too, had watched her grown children hurt by the loss of the sudden death of their father. "As for me, the son of a bitch couldn't keep his dick in his pants. He cheated on me endlessly." Jess felt uneasy. She shifted her weight on her heels and she could feel her face redden to her hairline.

"Oh gosh," she spoke. *What the hell else was she supposed to say? She had been one of those women who allowed Patrick Robertson between her thighs. Had Patrick really been with that many other women?*

Patrick's wife continued, "His latest fling was serious though. He was ready to leave me for her. He wanted a divorce." Jess swallowed hard. She wished more than anything right now that this woman would just hand over the suit on a hanger that she held draped over one arm. Jess wanted to take it and bolt back down the stairs with it. She would dress his body and then leave. Someone else could handle the rest of the preparations. She had done enough. Patrick's wife, however, had more to say. "I was told it was a one-car accident, en route to the backroads… near your home actually."

Jess froze.

"So, tell me, did you reject him? Is that why my husband is dead?"

Jess felt as if she was backed into a corner now.

"What are you implying?" Jess would attempt ignorance and denial before she would admit to this.

"Patrick never told me. I do have friends all over the Twin Cities though. And one happens to work for the florist who prepared the dozen red roses that my husband gave to you."

She won. The pretty redhead, Patrick's widow, had the upper hand. There was no denying this accusation now.

"He pursued me, yes, but I... the day he died in the car accident, I told him to go back to you and his children."

"So you didn't want him anymore?" her response was snarky. "Please. No need to act innocent. I know you were fucking him."

Jess made fleeting eye contact from this woman to the floor. And then she realized that she needed to own up to her actions. "I was sleeping with your husband, yes. I wish it had never happened. I wish Patrick had not died. I cannot take back my choices, but I do wonder about his choice on the backroads that day." She probably should not have said that, but the person to be angry at here was Patrick. He was to blame for being a coward. He should have gone back to save his marriage, and to keep his family together. Any sadness that Jess felt now turned to anger.

This time Patrick's wife stayed silent. She allowed what Jess had said to wash over her. She was either taken aback, or just startled that someone else may have thought it too. And, like Jess, she found the courage to speak her mind.

"No one is certain that Patrick did this to himself. Excessive speed. Lost control. Those are the terms used. Suicide is being left out to spare our feelings. Not yours, but rather mine, and his children, and his father left behind to grieve. No one has any clue that Patrick could have taken his own life because he was rejected by his whore. Between us, though, he didn't. I received a text from him just minutes before Patrick crashed his car, and he said, 'I'm coming home.'"

The suit for the corpse was aggressively thrown from the arms of Patrick's widow directly at Jess before she turned in her ballet flats and eventually slammed the door behind her.

By no lie or stretch of the imagination, Jess had been Patrick Robertson's whore. Now, she also turned on her heels and made her way back downstairs to dress the body of a man that would be soon be buried. He would never have another chance to make things right or feel remorseful for the hurt he caused. But Jess would. And she believed it was time she took that oath and changed her ways once and for all.

Chapter 16

Afton waited until after 5 p.m. to leave the studio. She wondered what she would find when she got home. Had Skye stayed there after she relieved Dylan from helping with the baby? Or perhaps Knox was home again with both of the girls. There was no communication exchange between them today, and Afton didn't like the way that felt at all. She was used to a text or a quick phone call from him.

Only Knox's car was on the driveway when Afton parked beside it. She grabbed her camera bag and her laptop and made her way inside.

The baby was asleep in the swing in the middle of the living room, while her big sister watched TV. Afton greeted Bella with a kiss on top of that dark head of hair while she stared at the TV. The baby still had rosy cheeks, but looked content as she slept in motion.

Knox was in the kitchen when Afton walked through the doorway. He still had his work clothes on, but his shirt was untucked. He was rummaging through the refrigerator.

"Hi," Afton spoke first. She hated the tension between them.

Knox acknowledge her with eye contact, and then spoke. "I am looking for something to cook for dinner." He and Bella had just gotten home, and then Skye left.

"I haven't given it any thought. Do you just want to order take-out? Bella will eat pizza." She knew that about her niece. She held onto that silly tidbit of information and stated it as fact to reinstate her place in her life. Much unlike last night when Afton wanted no part of claiming either of them. *They weren't her responsibility.* But yet they were because she loved them — as well as her sister, and Knox. *What had she been thinking?* She hadn't. They were both overtired and utterly stressed from the day's events.

Knox closed the refrigerator door before he responded. "Or maybe Chinese. That way she will eat some vegetables and rice." Knox was being the responsible one. Afton nodded.

It was Afton's turn to walk over to the refrigerator. She took out a bottle of water and twisted off the cap. Knox stood near the counter. "Was Skye here today?"

"Yes, for awhile, before she took Blair to the pediatrician to get her checked out. She's fine. The fever and runny nose could be from teething."

"Good," Afton replied. "I wondered if she would take the girls back home tonight, you know, because they aren't feeling well."

"Blair no longer has a fever. And besides, I can handle both of them when they aren't feeling well." Knox was offended. *Shit. That came out wrong. What Afton really wanted to say to him was... I'm sorry about last night.*

"I know you can," Afton responded, but that was all she said. She kept silent now. She said things that were too difficult to take back and the damage was already done. What pained her most was Knox had his walls up. He had stopped trying to reach her. He was the communicator. *What's going on? Why did you say the things you said? Let's work this out. It's us...we can overcome anything.*

~

Afton helped with the girls all evening. She played the Memory board game with Bella as many times as she wanted. And she picked up and held Blair every time she so much as whimpered. She of course loved those girls and, yes, she was trying very hard to send a message to Knox.

She was sitting on their bed while Knox showered. She prepared her apology in her mind. But when he came out of the bathroom, wearing only navy pajama bottoms, she wasn't the one who spoke first.

"I think I'll sleep in the spare bedroom tonight, just to be closer to the girls, so I can hear if they need anything through the night."

Afton felt her chest fall. This hurt. The thought of being apart from him was unimaginable. "Don't. Don't do this, Knox." He turned to her. His hair was still damp from the shower. "We'll hear them. This isn't about listening for the girls. You're angry with me, and you are punishing me by distancing yourself."

"I'm not angry," he clarified. "I'm disappointed. We are supposed to be in this together. And suddenly you are telling me that my baby is mine and Skye's responsibility. You are their aunt. And you are going to be my wife. Why can't you see that your role in their lives is significant!" He was definitely angry. *But Afton did like how he still wanted her to be his wife.*

"I'm not denying any of that," she began. "It's the way you went about informing me that if Blair was sick and not able to go to daycare the following day, well, I had to stay home. No one asked me if I had scheduled clients. You are a doctor. And Skye had an entire convention center waiting to hear her speak. I am just a photographer. Or so that's how you made me feel."

"Afton, that's not what I meant. Not at all."

"No? Sam used to demean me. He'd ask if I had any measly pictures to take again. My career for so very long was my passion. It still is in many ways. He never did understand that." Afton hadn't expected to admit any of that to Knox, but she felt desperate now.

"I would never degrade you or your successful career. If a bad memory of Sam caused you to shut down like you did, then you need to talk to me. From my perspective, I saw someone who's very much a part of this equation, this uniquely blended family, act as if you weren't."

"I did," Afton admitted. "I immediately wanted to place the ball back in your court. Your baby, your problem. That was wrong of me. I'm sorry. I reacted badly because I felt less important." Afton still felt ashamed of her actions last night, but a part of her believed they were warranted.

"Important?" Knox questioned her. "I have a baby now. And she, and her big sister, are the most important people in my life. I will always be there for them. And you… Afton, you not only are vital to my being, you are my life. Nothing matters half as much to me if I cannot share it with you. My body. My soul. My heart. My life. I spoke to you as my other half when I mentioned needing help with my child, because I consider her to be yours too."

Afton wiped away tears. *Damn it! She hated to cry.* There was something more she wanted to say to him. She wasn't the only one at fault in this argument. He had hurt her as well. "I chose to be with Jess all evening, and I know you had your hands full with the girls, but you seemed upset with me for not being here. You made light of my relationship with her. She's my best friend, she needed me, and I wanted to be there for her. I think your comments about her set me off. We were both tired and just done with a very long day. So, for my part in that, I'm sorry."

"You're right. We both said some things we shouldn't have. I'm sorry I let that happen." Afton watched him finally move from the middle of their bedroom. He sat on the bed bedside her.

"This is hard," she admitted. "Sharing a life with someone is not easy. We know this because, circumstances aside, we both failed at it before. I don't want to give up on us, ever. I guess this is how it feels when the honeymoon stage is over." She attempted to laugh, but she didn't think it was all that funny.

"Hey… who said *that* has to end? Knox leaned toward her to kiss her, but she pulled away.

"I'm just being real. The passion will fade one day. We have our hands full here as we build a life together. We have, as you put it, a uniquely blended family. I believe our love is strong enough to bend through anything. I know that. I would never have gone this far with you if I didn't."

He exhaled in relief. "I believe that, too."

"Then what are we doing?" she asked him.

"Making up… I hope," he moved closer to her again.

"You can kiss me now," she gave him a come-hither look that he never wanted more than he did right at this moment.

He pressed his lips to hers with force. There was desperation and rejuvenated energy between them. They were a couple. They were a unit who needed to be together, or the other would not feel whole. *Soul mates.* He looked into her eyes. And she had never felt more wanted. Or desired. Or loved.

Chapter 17

After two weeks in the hospital, Liam was discharged. The doctor warned him that continued rest was still vital to his recovery. Because he had previously been diagnosed with popcorn lung, portions of his airways would have a lifelong obstruction which would prevent him from a complete recovery. Liam continued to battle a cough, shortness of breath, wheezing, and just feeling tired. Laney and Brad had also reached the point of exhaustion.

Fourteen nights had passed in the hospital, where either Brad or Laney stayed all night long with their son. This was the first time their family of four was under the same roof in weeks. It was a reason to celebrate. Liam had survived a freak accident and pneumonia that settled in his already compromised lungs. He was under the care of his brother now, as his parents retreated to their bedroom, to a bed they had not shared in weeks.

It felt strange, yet familiar. Uneasy, yet comfortable. The last time they laid side by side in their bed like this, Brad had given Laney an ultimatum. Get help, or get out. She did neither. Their son's crisis had forced her to just stop drinking. Cold turkey. Abruptly she had quit. With no counseling or medical help. Ironically, that was what Brad had believed she could have done all along. *Just stop drinking!* It hadn't been easy, and Laney still wanted a drink. *Daily. Nightly. Multiple times around the clock.* In a way, Laney also felt like she had been released today. Not so much from hospitalization, but more like confinement from the real world. A world where she needed a drink sometimes just to take the edges off the day. *So what happens now?* Laney wished she knew.

They were lying side by side in total darkness. "We are so lucky to have our boy home," Laney spoke. She wasn't ready to close her eyes and drift off to sleep. Her body begged to differ, but her mind was still reeling. She needed to talk to her husband. They had avoided this conversation for weeks.

"He's going to be okay, Lane. You heard the doctor. Yes, his lungs aren't a hundred percent, but he's a young, resilient boy with a future."

She sighed in the dark. "Thank God for that."

Brad turned toward her. He propped himself up on his elbow. "And thank you." She turned to him as she waited for him to go on, to clarify what he wanted to tell her. "I am so proud of you. All on your own, you did it." He never spoke the words *drinking* or *alcohol*. Laney of course knew why. Her addiction had affected him too. In the worst way. She had felt lost to him.

"It's hard, Brad." And she didn't know if her feat was entirely accomplished. *Was this really over? Was she considered to be a recovering alcoholic?* She had indeed gone through the most difficult part. The withdrawal headaches had finally subsided. At one point she questioned Liam's doctor, in confidence, if ibuprofen was addictive. *It wasn't.* She also had turned to food to more frequently to fill the void for alcohol. Being stuck in that hospital meant she had gotten very little exercise which already changed her body in recent weeks. She felt chunky and unattractive. She missed her old, familiar self.

"You made it through," he spoke, confident that because Laney had given up drinking, all would be right in their world again. His naivety about this frustrated her. What he couldn't understand was that she still wanted to a drink. The temptation was still there. But Laney kept quiet because Brad believed in her. On the surface, she was the strongest person he ever knew. She didn't need a half a dozen weeks in a rehabilitation clinic. She hadn't chosen alcohol over him. Their marriage was solid again, their family was intact. All was right in Brad Potter's world. But his wife was still quietly unraveling.

"This still feels very much like a one day at a time thing for me," she admitted. Brad touched her now. His open palm rested on the side of her face. For weeks in their son's hospital room they had given each other comforting hugs and held hands when the doctor spoke of things like prognosis and a lifelong condition.

"I can't say that I am able to wrap my brain around how that must feel," he admitted, but just know that it's okay to crave a drink. That doesn't mean you're weak or about to fail. Just don't do it, Lane. Okay?" *If only it were that easy.* Laney just nodded her head as if she had to be the compliant, good wife. She would press on and try her damndest to keep the temptation at bay. She had to. Or she would lose her husband.

Brad traced his fingers on her jawline, down her neck, and onto her collarbone. He moved aside the thin straps of her nightgown. He leaned in to kiss her bare shoulder. She closed her eyes. This was her husband. Their attraction had always been wild and passionate. They couldn't get enough of each other. Always. That had not changed in the two decades that they had been together. "I love you," she heard him whisper. "I want you so much."

He touched her. He kissed her full on the mouth and all over her body. This was slow, sensual lovemaking. Laney still responded to him, physically. Her body craved his hands and mouth and his manhood. She wanted him inside her. But her mind was not into this. It was almost as if she was outside of her own body, watching and thinking about what those two people were doing to each other in that bed. And when it was over, she heard Brad ask her something he never had following sex. "Are you okay, babe?"

"Of course," she answered before she kissed his lips and then turned her back to him with tears welling up in her eyes.

∼

Dylan Fruend had a bag packed and placed near the front door of his home. It was a sizeable weathered leather duffel bag that Skye had come to love as a symbol of all the nights they spent together when he stayed with her and the girls. She looked forlorn as she watched him. "I thought you would be happy to be rid of me for a couple nights," he winked at her. She wished she could have gone along with him. A weekend getaway in St. Louis appealed to her. But tonight she would have her girls back, as she had missed them for three days while they were bonding and making memories with their daddy and Afton. Bella had recently began calling Knox her daddy. Afton told Skye of the special moment when Bella asked Knox if she could call him daddy like her baby sister would one day when she learned to talk. Skye would be forever grateful for all that Knox Manning had brought into their lives. He was her sister's great love. He was, first, a father figure to Bella and now the real thing. And by the grace of timing and circumstance he was Blair's biological father.

"Never," she wrapped her arms around his neck. They were almost eye-level. If she had been wearing heels, they would be. "Tell me again what's so important about this convention in St. Louis?"

Dylan paused. It wasn't a convention. Dr. Wesley Wright, PhD., a cell biologist at Saint Louis University had responded to the inquiry about his remarkable success story as a multiple myeloma survivor. They were going to meet in person. Dr. Wright had agreed once Dylan told him about Skye. A patient he had fallen in love with. A middle-aged woman who had two small daughters to raise. The fact that a remission had come on the heels of her myeloma diagnosis fascinated Dr. Wright. Every case certainly was not alike.

"It's not a convention. Just a consultation with a college professor. He specializes in cell biology research, and honestly his own medical story fascinates me. I've spent my career always looking for more knowledge. This trip is about gaining more insight so I can help my patients to the best of my ability." He was a leave-no-stone-unturned kind of man. And Skye was the patient that he would go to the ends of the earth for. Dylan was not ready to share any of the specifics with her just yet. He had too many unanswered questions still.

"You'll have to tell me about him sometime, his medical story, I mean."

"I will definitely do that," Dylan pulled her closer and kissed her goodbye for now.

Chapter 18

Saint Louis University was the oldest university west of the Mississippi River. Dylan Fruend could feel the history on that campus. Anything that existed since the late 1800s was sacred. There were 131 buildings housed on 235 acres of land, and Dylan found the middle point known as the clock tower. From there, he discovered the location of the Doisy Research Center — which was where Dr. Wright's office was located.

There was no secretary or lobby. It was just a closed door at the end of a long hallway. The nameplate read Dr. Wesley Wright, PhD. Dylan tapped his knuckles on the door twice, and immediately he heard, "come on in," from the opposite side of that door. Dylan turned the handle and stepped into a reasonably sized office with a desk in the middle and a couch against the far wall. The view of the campus from a large window sans curtains or blinds caught his eye. And a man, shorter in height in comparison to an average 6-foot-tall male, stood up from behind his desk. He certainly had the look of a professor. Or at least Dylan remembered more than a few from medical school who fit the description. Khaki pants. Checkered dress shirt. Dark rimmed glassed. In this case, Dr. Wright had a chain attached to his eyeglasses and they dangled around his neck at the moment. He was small-boned, skinny, with dark graying hair and a mustache that was twisted on the sides. His smiled was wide. "You must be Dr. Fruend?"

Dylan extended his hand. "Yes, but please call me Dylan."

"And I'm Wesley. I have to say I've never had anyone travel far and wide to meet with me." Those who wanted to pick his brain regarding being cured from a rare blood cancer had either been in his circle, or contacted him by phone or email. Ten years ago there wasn't the advantage of social media. And it had been four years since Wesley was cured of myeloma. Dylan sat down on one of the two chairs in front of the professor's desk, and he watched Wesley find a comfortable corner on that desk. He was in close proximity to Dylan as if he was ready to give him undivided attention. "You're here because you've become personally invested in saving one of your patients."

Dylan nodded. "You were cured of myeloma. I've discovered many cases through the years of my medical career that were unexplainable, but yours was different. You aren't just one of those beat-all-the-odds, walking miracles. You publicly shared the tools for how you did this. I felt compelled to contact you and I'm sitting here right now because I want to—"

"Do the same for the woman you love?" Wesley interjected.

"Yes," Dylan answered without hesitation.

"I didn't know I had a deadly disease pulsing through my veins until one day I sneezed and I broke a vertebra that had been damaged by the cancer. The myeloma nearly did me in. I'll give it to you straight. I won't waste your time telling you it was not that bad, or it seemed like a lifetime ago and I've forgotten the measly details. None of that is true. I was 37 years old and my doctors treated the cancer vigorously for over a decade. Until they were out of options. I was then told to prepare to die, to get the help of hospice to make my last days comfortable. You know all about the hopeless feeling of telling your patients those final words." Dylan nodded, and continued to listen raptly. Already, this man intoxicated him. He was genuine. His intelligence and eloquence saturated his every word or gesture. Or, maybe none of that was true? Perhaps Dylan Fruend had created a myth of a man in his own mind before he ever stepped off that airplane at Lambert International in the City of St. Louis. He certainly had put every ounce of his faith into him having the answers to save Skye's life.

"Having cancer was completely unexpected because I felt fine," Wesley continued. "The real challenge for me became the research. I began to study the disease and this form of cancer. I learned there was not a single drug in the pipeline that was going to help me and that there hadn't been any new drugs in the field in over three decades. So the hard part for me was that I was stunned."

"But not stunned to the point of acceptance," Dylan noted. "What I mean is, you literally refused to lay down and die." It was a hurrah in his favor that was well-deserved. The man saved his own life because he had not given up on sifting through all of the possibilities. Even the ones no one else had the balls to give a try.

"Never once did I accept defeat, which was why I jumped at the chance to be a lab rat, so to speak. There are clinical trials all the time for everything, and I opted to be one of those subjects. What did I have to lose? My life? Well that was already up for grabs. I was the recipient of a living drug made by extracting some of my own immune cells and genetic code to recognize and defeat the cancer."

"I understand this as your DNA and your own cancer-infested cells were programmed to kill all cancerous cells labeled with this particular marker, or antigen — like when a common cold virus causes the body to make antibodies and helps to prevent the person from getting sick."

Wesley nodded. "Correct. This was a radical departure from all medicines to date."

"And the end result was a cure." Dylan couldn't conceal the smile that widened on his face.

"But not without its challenges, and those challenges remain for patients today as they did for me a few years ago. The regimen is incredibly complicated, and each treatment costs hundreds of thousands of dollars." Dylan had known that the cell regimen left researchers unsure how to make it a widespread, standard part of myeloma treatment. He had not, however, known about the complications, or challenges, as Wesley had put it. That was another reason why he was there today. He needed to know what this would put Skye through.

"In a 21-patient trial, 71 percent will see complications when the weaponized cells cause what is known as a cytokine storm, where the cancer cells die all at once, along with the cells created in this living drug. That complete destruction releases substances that cause inflammation. That has led to miserable flu-like symptoms, fever, and low blood pressure which has resulted in life-threatening organ damage."

"Give me the statistics," Dylan requested.

"Seventy-one percent of patients experienced that cytokine release syndrome where most cases were mild to moderate. Eighty-six percent had serious blood count problems that can lead to infection. Fifty-seven percent had existing anemia," Dylan thought of Skye, "and that already low blood cell count plummeted. Forty-three percent developed a low blood platelet level. And 21 percent had neurotoxicity, which was damage to the brain or nervous system."

"You have to consider the risks, I get that," Dylan spoke up.

"And you're asking your patient, or in your case the woman you love, to take them."

"It's dangerous. That's what you're telling me," Dylan noted.

"I didn't see the danger in it. For me, it was one last chance I had to live. Every patient is different. I must say, Skye Gallant's case is a rarity. She was diagnosed through a routine a blood test and told the myeloma was present. And she maintains a remission status, correct?"

Dylan nodded his head. "It's been fourteen months of the same. Anemia is a factor, but now controlled by medication."

"So this, your being here today, is merely preparation for a time, if or when, something changes."

"I think I'd be a damn fool if I didn't have a plan in place. You said so yourself that your medical team had exhausted its plan. A chemotherapy regimen had brought you to death's door regardless."

"You're thinking with the live drug, you will spare her years of pumping that poison into her body for it to possibly not even be effective," Wesley made the obvious conclusion.

"From the moment I met her, I've never stopped thinking about how and why she was placed into my life. For reasons unknown? Perhaps. Or, I choose to believe it's because I can save her."

"Not you," Wesley clarified, "the living drug. The regimen that she will be put through. That's what has the potential to save her life. You will just be the man who held her hand and led her to a cure."

Hearing those promising words aloud, outside of his own mind, empowered Dylan Fruend. He was face to face with a man who was a medical miracle, who could explain precisely why and how he was cured of myeloma. This wasn't false hope. This wasn't crazy thinking in the midst of being so in love with a woman that he could not differentiate real from fantasy. He was confident —statistics and risks aside— that he was going to be ready and armed for the day Skye's cancer relapsed.

ten months later

Chapter 19

There were birthday balloons tied to the mailbox and blowing in the wind outside of the house on Holly Avenue. Blair Manning turned one year old. Her entire family gathered to celebrate the baby girl who changed their lives.

Afton was delighted to have her grown children there. Her son, Latch brought his partner with him. He was in a new relationship and Afton was supportive. This was the first time she had met Trey, and she liked him. She liked him because her son looked happy by his side. And that was all that mattered. Afton was proud of her family, every last one of them, for welcoming the couple into their family circle. There was no room for judgement in any of their hearts. Her daughter, Amy came alone with her fourteen-month-old son, Greyson Samuel. Her fiancé had to work and would be late to the party. Afton hoped the reason for his tardiness was true, but she and her daughter had not been close in a very long time. She wouldn't confide in her if there was something wrong. Afton scooped up Greyson and embraced him. He giggled and was content for a long while in his granny's arms. Afton briefly thought of Sam and wondered what kind of grandfather he would have been to his namesake. Probably a doting one. But, that, they would never know.

Dylan Fruend was there with Skye and her girls. It was a celebration he would not have missed for anything. Skye's daughters felt like his own. And this family was unlike one he had ever known. He wanted to be a part of it officially one day. But, for now, he and Skye were over the moon happy just being in love and sharing their lives together. It had actually felt like they were already married.

Laney and Brad and the boys were there. Both Liam and Luke were attached to their phones. A one-year-old birthday party wasn't exactly their idea of a fun time. Liam had finally gotten out of his slump, as he had spent the past few months dwelling on his heartbreak. Shey had broken up with him when a college boy, three years older than her, had shown an interest in her. Laney had felt terribly sorry for him, but she also discreetly rejoiced in the triumph of being rid of that girl who had a hold on her son for far too long. Laney reached between her boys now to retrieve their empty soda cans on the sofa table. She also reached for someone's empty glass with partially melted ice and a beer can. As she juggled it all, she stepped toward the kitchen. No one was near her, or watching. She was used to being discreet these days. And she had to stay in control, or Brad would find out. She opened the pantry door in the kitchen to recycle the aluminum cans. She dropped the soda cans in first, and saved the beer can for last. There was some liquid swishing around in the bottom of it, a good swallow at least. It didn't matter whose it was. Laney pressed the can to her lips and tipped it back. She didn't even like beer. But quick alcohol fixes were how she coped now. She brushed her teeth often, or chewed gum afterward. Brad was oblivious. It was risky, Laney knew all too well, but without the smallest amount of alcohol in her system, she was numb. Nothing in her life had felt the same or made her happy. Consequently, she had reverted back to being a closet drinker.

The party was winding down and so was the guest of honor. Skye noted that Blair missed her nap, and asked Knox if she could lay her down in her crib upstairs. He was on her heels with a blanket left behind as Blair couldn't fall asleep without it.

When Skye turned away from placing Blair into her crib, she wasn't settled. She wouldn't lay down until Knox came to a quick rescue with the blanket.

Skye's face lit up as she glanced from Knox to Blair. "Oh look what daddy has! Your blankie!" Knox exaggerated a sprint straight for the crib and Blair squealed behind that loose pacifier in her mouth. *So much for winding down a one-year-old for a much-needed nap.* Even still, those two were adorable together.

She watched Knox scoop up his baby girl into his arms. She curled her body against his chest. He held her with the most gentle, loving arms. The two of them were bonded forever and always. Skye's eyes were misty. He kissed the top of her head multiple times. He tousled her caramel brown hair. "It's sleepy time, birthday girl. I hope you had a happy day. You make daddy so happy by just being mine." Skye thought about the phrasing of those special words. His daughter's mere existence had fulfilled him.

He placed her into the crib and laid her down on her back. She balled up and tightened the blanket to her chest, where Knox now placed his open palm. Without giving it a second thought, Skye placed her hand on top of Knox's. Their daughter stayed still as if she knew how special this moment was to be together with both of her parents.

Skye felt sentimental today, and especially during this moment with Knox. They had a shared a special year with their baby girl. She was growing and thriving between two homes. They were doing better than okay as a not-so-typical family.

Knox followed Skye out of nursery and softly closed the door behind him. "You okay?" He asked Skye in almost a whisper.

"I'm just taking it all in," she responded. "I'm here and so grateful to have lived the first year of Blair's life with her. Doing this shared parenting thing with you truly has been better than I ever imagined."

Knox's smile reached his eyes. He felt the depth of this. All of it. His dream to be a father came true, and Skye's continued good health was an endless prayer answered. "I'm forever indebted to you," Knox responded. He didn't say it enough. It was inappropriate to express around Afton. He was grateful to her, too. But it was Skye who ultimately allowed this miracle to happen.

Skye rolled her eyes. "Stop. Afton would make you sleep on the sofa if she heard you talking like that."

He didn't find the humor in that. "I'm not disrespecting her, not at all. This is a happy day for us. Blair has so many people in her life who love her. Dylan and Afton are very much like parents to our girls as well." *Our girls.* Skye was touched. This man was such a gift to the Gallant family.

"I want you to always remember something," Skye began. They were still standing in the upstairs hallway just outside of the closed door of Blair's nursery. "If God takes me from this world and away from those girls... I know you've got this. Your bond with both of them is solid. The love that you share with them is a comfort to me now... and it will be then, if—"

"There's no sense in talking like that. You're going to outlive all of us," Knox would bargain with God for that to be true if it were possible.

"Just hear me when I say that I'm grateful for you, Knox Manning."

"Back at you, Skye Gallant." He winked at her.

∼

Dylan was at the bottom of the stairway when he watched Skye begin to descend it with Knox only a step or two behind her. Dylan tipped a bottle of water to his mouth. He had a beer earlier, which he thought he left unfinished on the sofa table, but it was gone. He could never take his eyes off Skye. Her lengthy legs. Her long blonde hair. Her beauty was striking. Her personality drew him in from the moment they met. She was witty. She was loud. She was smart. And she was beautiful. Dylan was instantly startled from his thoughts of her when he saw her miss the third to last step. She started to fall forward when he lunged toward her. "Skye!"

Knox attempted to grab ahold of her, but she fell into Dylan instead. Her head tilted back in the crick of his arm. He heard the commotion of Skye's sisters behind him as they were making their way to her. He had her though. He laid her flat on her back at the base of the stairs. She was unconscious, but her vitals were strong. "Call for an ambulance," Dylan instructed clearly. In just a few days Skye was due again for a complete round of blood work. Her diagnosis of myeloma had remarkably been in remission for almost two years.

Chapter 20

The house on Holly Avenue was empty now. The birthday balloons were still attached to the mailbox but were nearing deflation. The party was over. Knox stayed behind to be with Bella and Blair. Someone had to, and those girls were his responsibility, as Afton and Laney followed the ambulance that Dylan rode along in with Skye. She only briefly regained consciousness, so the paramedics were quick to move her to seek further medical attention at the hospital.

Knox thought about the conversation he just shared with Skye. It was almost as if she had an inkling that something was going to happen. It scared him to think that it could be serious this time. He waited now for Afton to call him when she knew something about Skye. *His girls needed their mother. He needed her, too. They were co-parents for life.*

~

Skye fully regained consciousness in the ambulance on the way to the hospital. Dylan calmed her when she wanted to panic and ask too many questions. Or make assumptions. They wouldn't know anything until he got a complete blood draw from her and rushed it through the lab.

There were three stages of myeloma and the higher the stage, the poorer the outcome. Nearly two years ago, Skye was diagnosed as having Stage 1, and had not required treatment. She also was classified as being in Group A versus Group B because her kidneys still had normal function. Her blood count continued to show abnormalities in the blood cells. She also still had a high level of protein in her blood and urine. Those results had not altered significantly over the two-year period. The only thing that had changed for Skye was being anemic. All of those things were under Dylan's watchful eye as the remission continued. This time, however, the CBC order of Skye's blood showed considerable changes. The cancer was active.

It was time for Dylan to get back to Skye. He had only left her for what he said would be a few minutes. She knew he was going to read her test results. She was impatient for him to return, and afraid of the news he would have for her. Dylan pushed himself to put one foot in front of the other in the corridors from his office to the cubicle in the emergency room where Skye anticipated his return. He avoided the waiting room area where he knew Afton and Laney would be camped out until they heard some news. He told himself that this was his turf. Much like a coach on the court, he was in control and needed to display confidence and trust in his own skills. Skye was counting on him to guide her. And, yes, he did have a plan of immediate action.

When he walked into the room where Skye sat upright on the gurney, she noticed his blue eyes. There was always sincerity in them. That quality, she believed, made him a likeable guy and a trusted physician. He was as genuine as they come. But those eyes this time told a different story. *Sadness. Worry. Apprehension.* Skye already knew he didn't have good news for her.

He sat down on the edge of the gurney, and brushed against her. "How are you holding up?" he asked her.

"You tell me," she stated. "It's not good this time is, it? My blood work has changed. Give it to me straight, Fruend." This was the woman he fell for. *Don't mess around. Don't sugarcoat it.* She could handle it. He was counting on that more than she knew.

"The myeloma has reached Stage 2," was all he said at first. And that was enough. Skye swallowed hard the lump that had instantly risen from her chest to her throat. Her levels, at Stage 1, had been close to normal. The status of the genetic makeup of the cancer cells didn't make it overly aggressive. The cancer in her blood had been most treatable at that stage. Or, in her case, it was in some sort of lengthy remission. But her luck had run out.

"Which means I'm no longer in remission." It wasn't a question. It was a statement that she had spoken with very little emotion in her voice. Defeat was primarily what he heard. And Dylan Fruend wasn't having it.

"It's time to fight like a Gallant girl," he tried to shape a smile.

He watched tears form in her eyes. "I have two girls to win this fight for," she paused, "and you. I want more time together." She already had allowed herself to imagine growing old with him. He would never have visible gray hair, as his head was clean shaven. Father time would go easy on him that way. She tried to envision him older, or more distinguished as men seemed to get as they aged, but she couldn't. That scared her. For reasons unknown, she feared she would not be granted the privilege of living a long life.

He nodded his head. "That a girl. We've got this. I am right here, and I will not leave your side." He held her hand. Skye trusted him with her life.

"I'm scared, Dylan. I'm not as tough as I pretend to be."

He smiled a little. "None of us are." He was breaking inside right now. He wanted nothing more than to take this awful disease away from her, to make it completely disappear. To save her life. It's the reason their paths had crossed. He was sure of it.

"Seven years at best," she stated out of context, or at least Dylan had not followed her. He waited for more. "Stage 2 myeloma, with vigorous treatment, will prolong a patient's life for several years."

"You've done some research," he noted, and refrained to remind her that every case was different.

"Just tell me what I have to do. Lead the way. I don't want to think too much."

"A typical start would be to plan a chemotherapy regimen." That word stung her. It was poison, and only a way to prolong death. *Was that really what she wanted for herself? To be sick and weak and frail just to be kept alive, to buy time. What kind of mother could she be to Bella and Blair in that physical state?*

"What if I said no?" she asked him. "What if I just wanted to soak up what I have left of feeling just as I do right now. Not awful. And strong enough to get by."

"Decline treatment?" he asked her, feeling somewhat taken aback. She had just said she was ready to fight the cancer with all she had to give. Skye nodded to confirm his assumption. "I would not recommend sitting back and doing nothing to prevent the spread of the cancer. I do agree with you though... no chemotherapy."

Skye wore a look of confusion. "What? If not chemo, then what do I have to endure to get well?" She was at least back in the mindset of being proactive in this fight. She was the mother of young children. There would be no such thing as just sitting back and allowing the cancer to destruct.

"A clinical trial has been proven successful. It's more of a personalized therapeutic approach with a living drug that's created when your own cells are collected. Your own DNA and your own cancer-infested cells could be programmed to kill all of the cancer cells."

"Does something like that really work?" *And if it did, why wasn't everyone doing it? Why was there even a market, so to speak, for chemotherapy?*

"It's been proven to cure myeloma."

"I want to jump on this, I want to say, yes, let's do it! But there have to be risks or something that's keeping everyone from doing this living drug thing."

"It's really complex and researchers have yet to make this widespread. It's expensive, it also has its risks."

"What exactly would I be put through, I mean, how will my cells be extracted from my body? A blood draw?" Dylan was ready for these questions. Skye was far from being a medical mind, but she was intelligent and inquisitive and was always one to ask the right questions. Sometimes, those were the questions everyone else was thinking but not bold enough to put out there.

"The cells are removed by taking whole blood through a dialysis-like machine that spins off the targeted cells and returns the rest of the blood components to the patient. The collected cells expand in the lab and are infused back into the patient's circulatory system. If that is successful, the live drug concoction will multiply into an advancing army and take out all of the cancerous plasma cells by bursting the membranes, and consequently putting the patient into remission."

"I'm not sure that I understand all of that in its entirety," Skye admitted, "but I know you and if you believe this can work, I will agree to it. I mean, I still don't know the risks or the complications of it, but chemotherapy doesn't guarantee my life either. How many other patients of yours have you tried this living drug with?"

Dylan paused for a moment. "None. I discovered this successful regimen after you and I met. There's a cell biologist who battled myeloma for ten years. He was at the end of his life-saving possibilities. He was dying. He took a chance with the clinical trial, just in its beginning stages then, and he survived and has been cancer-free for almost five years. It cured him, Skye. I met this man. I spoke at length with him about all of it. You are a good candidate, Skye. This man's body went through years of treatment trauma. Yours has not. You would be going into this healthier and stronger than most."

"You always said you would take care of me," she noted. "You've done all of this for me? You had this plan of action in place all along, haven't you?"

"It's never left my mind. Don't misunderstand, you are not some sort of science experiment for me. I've rejoiced every single time your blood work showed remission status. But, as a doctor, I had to be realistic. This is cancer."

"Tell me about the complications. Will my hair fall out like yours?"

He smiled. "No. I'm the only one in this relationship who's going to be bald." She giggled. And she was relieved. Sure, her head of long, blonde, beautiful hair should be the least of her concerns, but she was human, she was a woman. *She liked her damn hair.* "I could recite some statistics to you," he began, "but the bottom line is no matter what we do with you is a risk. You could experience mild to moderate flu symptoms from inflammation. Fevers need to be kept under control to prevent organ damage. Blood count issues can occur, which have to be watched closely for infection. Low platelet levels can mess with the brain and nervous system. These are all things for me to worry about. Not you. Just trust me."

Skye nodded. He was still seated beside her on the gurney. She reached for him and touched his face. "I do trust you — with my life." He leaned into her and kissed her full and hard on the mouth. *She put all of her faith in him, she depended on him, and Dylan would never let her down.*

Chapter 21

It felt like hours before Afton and Laney could get to her. Their baby sister was sitting on a gurney with her knees pulled up to her chest. She was still wearing her birthday party clothes — flared faded jeans and a sleeveless cherry red blouse. *Red. She was the firecracker of the three of them. She was the one who took chances and figured it out later.*

Dylan left them alone in the cubicle to give them some time together. Somehow he knew both of Skye's sisters would have plenty to say to him later. And they would have every right to question his actions, or even his sanity. It would stem from how much they loved their sister. He understood that. He loved her too.

They took turns pulling her into tight hugs, as they expressed how much she scared everyone when she passed out on the stairs.

"How are my little girls?" Skye immediately asked what was on her mind.

"Knox has them at home," Afton told her, and Skye smiled. Of course they were in good hands. She really never doubted that.

"I need to tell you two what's going on with me," she began, and they both stood very still and close on one side of the gurney. "I've been promoted to Stage 2 of myeloma."

"Don't make light of something so serious," Afton scolded her as only a big sister would. Laney stayed silent. She was the middle sister who struggled to get a word in at times. The oldest always knew best…and the youngest was the focal point of all the attention.

"This is where it gets real," Skye noted. "I'm no longer considered to be in remission."

"You'll need treatment," Laney finally spoke. She imagined the havoc that chemotherapy would wreak on her sister's beautiful body.

Skye did not confirm or deny that she would begin a chemotherapy regimen. She only began talking to them. "Do you two remember when the fair came to town? I was 10 years old." Then, Laney was 15 and Afton was 20. "Aft, you were in college, and Laney you were in high school."

"I was dating Brad," Laney smiled at the memory of him being her first and only boyfriend.

"And Afton was overly attached to the camera hanging around her neck like a tourist." They laughed at her, and Afton flipped them both off. They laughed harder. Afton included herself in their amusement this time.

"The ferris wheel was downtown Saint Paul. It was lit up and larger than life. I wanted to go for a ride on that with the two of you. I whined so much about it and you both eventually dropped everything and took me on it. Do you remember when it stopped and we were at the very top?"

Laney laughed. "We told you we were stuck and never getting down. We should have known better though. Things like that never did faze you, let alone scare you."

"I was with you both. Why would I be scared?" Afton and Laney caught themselves fighting back tears. "I remember looking across the entire town from up there, and wondering what was out there for me. Afton, you had career goals that put a fire in your soul. Laney, you had already met the love of your life. I was just a kid, still trying to figure it all out."

"But look at you now," Afton beamed. "A mother to two beautiful daughters. You're a girl mom, just like Hope Gallant once was." The mention of their mother's name brought such pride to each of them.

"And you found true love," Laney added, referring to Dr. Dylan Fruend.

Skye beamed. "He was worth the wait, and the screw-ups I made along the way."

"Everything that happens to us molds us into who we eventually become," Afton said, and she probably understood that more than any of them. She had lived years of her life in a failed marriage that inevitably taught her what not to do and how not to be in a relationship. Knox was her fresh start, her new beginning. She wasn't going to mess up her second chance.

"I see Dylan as entering my life at just the right time. I mean, come on, he's my doctor, a specialist for blood cancer. You want to talk about someone being all things to me — including a lifesaver!"

Afton and Laney both felt the same feeling at the moment. Skeptical. Not because they didn't like the guy. They were just being realistic. What if Dylan could not save their sister's life? They certainly would have hope and faith, but the possibility of something going wrong was apparently not even on Skye's radar.

"To see that you have him to count on for everything, including this fight you're up against with cancer, does feel fateful," Laney noted.

"What is his plan for your treatment?" Afton shifted gears back to being realistic. She didn't believe in doctors saving lives. Sure, they were the masterminds behind the research, the medicine and the treatments, but God ultimately decided who would live or die. She would not put that kind of pressure on any man.

"He wants to bypass chemotherapy. There's a proven, effective way to beat this with a live drug. I didn't retain all of the medical lingo that Dylan used, but samples of my DNA and my own cancerous cells will be taken from me through a dialysis-like procedure. Those cells will be joined in a lab and somehow programmed to kill all of the cancer cells once they are infused back into my circulatory system. It's a cure for myeloma. I will no longer have cancer once I complete the clinical trial."

"Trial? You mean like an experiment?" Afton spoke up, and Laney's eyes widened.

Skye shrugged.

"Don't shrug your shoulders like a careless teenager. This is your life we are talking about, a life that you seem to have so freely put into Dylan Fruend's hands without giving the guarantees a second thought."

"Guarantees? There are no guarantees with life. You should know that better than anyone."

"What's that supposed to mean?" Afton snapped back at Skye, and Laney had never felt more in the middle of those two than she had right now.

"I'm referring to Sam, the man who strutted around like he had the world by the ass, and then one day he fell off the face of the earth. As I said, there are no guarantees for any of us no matter how sure we are of ourselves or anything else."

Afton stayed quiet at first. "Right. I'm sorry. I just can't comprehend how you would agree to be a guinea pig when your life is at stake."

"I trust Dylan. He's been researching this. He tracked down a cell biologist who battled myeloma for more than a decade. He was at death's door when chemo failed him. He had nothing else to lose, so he tried the living drug treatment and it cured him. How could I not want to take that chance?"

"We understand," Laney spoke for both herself and Afton. "We're just worried about you, that's all. What are the ramifications if something goes wrong? Have you and Dylan discussed a backup plan?"

"When you have cancer it's a game changer," Skye attempted to explain. "It's a one day at a time affair. You don't concern yourself with what lies ahead. You just give it your all with what you've got in the moment." Skye paused before she finished saying what they both needed to hear. "When I found out that I was sick, I stopped at nothing to give Bella a sibling. I secured her future in that way. And now both of my girls also have a father. I have a plan in place for them. Everything else is bonus. Time spent with you two. Being in love with Dylan. It's all more special to me now than you can imagine."

"You always did take chances first and figure out the rest later," Afton noted what she always believed about her.

"I won't deny how that has worked for me time and again," Skye spoke. "But what's different for me now is I'm not alone. Finally, I'm not the one steering this ship through the rough waters with unforeseen danger. It's Dylan. When he came in here earlier with my blood draw results and he was trying to conceal the sadness in his eyes, I told him to just tell me what I have to do and lead me there, because I don't want to have to think too much."

Afton started to cry. *She hated to cry!* She turned her back and walked out of the room. Laney glanced in her direction and then back at Skye on the gurney, who didn't seem overly concerned about Afton's need to escape.

"Give her some time. She always comes around."

Chapter 22

Afton stood against the wall in the hallway adjacent to the chaos of the emergency room. She held her phone in her hands and texted Knox.

Skye's cancer is no longer in remission.

She placed her phone back inside her handbag, pushed her body away from the wall that was currently holding her up, and she made her way to Dylan Fruend's office.

She knocked as she turned the door handle and pushed open the door. Dylan watched her walk into his space on her own terms. He wasn't surprised by this. She was the protective older sister.

"Have a seat, Afton. I know you must be reeling from this news." They all were.

"I'll stand, thank you," she stated in almost a stubborn way. "I want you to know that I like you. I think you are so good for my sister, and her girls."

"But you don't trust that I know what I'm doing because what I'm suggesting seems drastic and careless. Don't you think that I know that? I've spent months researching and configuring the facts, the pros, the cons. I kept this information from Skye until I read the numbers from her blood work today, because I was not going to be the one to give her false hope or to put something in her head that she could fall back on with overconfidence each time she thought about this day when everything changed with just two words — rebounded remission."

"But you've gone ahead with this ludicrous plan anyway? Because why? What changed after a little time and research? Or did you just run out of time now that Skye is sick and you have to take action?"

"I don't take being a hematologist-oncologist that lightly," Dylan defended himself. "This method is a proven cure for myeloma. How can I turn my back on that? How can you?"

"Something could go wrong. This is my sister's life. That high medical status of yours has turned you into a cocky son of a bitch."

Dylan shook his head and actually concealed a chuckle. The Gallant girls were feisty fighters. Although there was very little physical resemblance between Afton and Skye —except for that bridge of freckles across their noses— Dylan could see what was very much alike about them now. "Something can go wrong anytime, anywhere. In the operating room. Being on a prescribed medication. Crossing the street without looking both ways for chrissakes!" He paused. He inhaled a deep breath and regained his calm. "Do you see what I'm saying? This is a chance to save Skye's life, to save her years of treatments that may or may not work. We have to do this."

"We? Are you referring to my resistance to support my sister in this risky decision?"

"No. I meant myself. She and I are in this together. I will be with her for every small step and for every hurdle. I'll be monitoring each tedious detail of the entire process. Saving your sister is my sole focus."

Afton started at him in silence, long and hard, before she turned around and left. Dylan could see in her eyes that he had gotten to her. She finally understood. This time, —the end goal, an attainable result within their reach— outweighed the risk.

~

Skye was admitted to Regional Minneapolis and would not leave the hospital until the cell regimen was complete. A medical team from Saint Louis University Hospital, where Wesley Wright had his success with the living drug regimen, were coming to Skye. Dylan had prearranged for this to happen. Myeloma was a disease of the plasma cells, the white blood cells found in the bone marrow that, as key parts of the immune system, made antibodies. It was important for Skye to stay clear of germs beforehand, which meant limited visitors. Even still, she insisted on Knox bringing her girls to see her. She missed them terribly. She did not have the mindset of goodbye. She would not go there, as it would be unbearable for her and confusing for them. She just wanted to see their faces, hold them and kiss them. They were her babies.

When Knox brought the girls to her, Afton gave the four of them some alone time together, while she stayed in the building and sat alone with a cup of tea. These days with her sister, leading up to the procedure that could cure the cancer in her blood, were emotionally exhausting for all of them.

Knox helped both of the girls up on the bed with Skye. They squealed and giggled, and Skye radiated absolute happiness to be with them again.

"Are you sick?" four-year-old Bella asked her mommy, and she studied her with a curiosity that Skye repeatedly had sworn she was born with.

"I am, but if I stay in the hospital for a little while longer, I will be all better and able to come home again."

"I miss our house," Bella spoke up. Knox smiled. It was remarkable how the girls had adapted to having two homes.

"I miss our house, too, and all of our things," Skye stated.

"We saw Dylan in the hallway. He said he misses us so much."

Skye smiled. "I know that is true because he talks about both of you all the time." Bella giggled, and Blair scooted closer to her mother. Skye touched their faces, combed her fingers through their hair and planted kisses on their soft skin. She inhaled their sweet scents and began to feel overcome with the intense emotion that she had pushed down deep and forced herself to ignore. *What if this was really the last time she held them and loved on them? What if she died and left them behind at one and four years old? Where would death take her? Would she be able to see them still? Hear them? Check on them, and keep them clear of danger? Or was heaven just too far away?*

Knox noticed Skye was struggling to keep herself together. "Girls, tell mommy what we have planned for when she gets better."

Bella was quick to chime in. She clearly was going to be the one always ready to speak first, like her mother. "We are all going to an indoor water park at a dodge."

"A lodge," Knox interjected to correct her.

"A l-odge," Bella was careful to repeat. "All of us are going! Dylan and Afton, too. Maybe even Laney and Brad, but Liam and Luke might not want to go. They are getting too big to have fun with kid stuff." Skye smiled. All of them together simply sounded nice.

"It will be a celebration," Knox stated, "for when you have this behind you."

Skye looked up at him and smiled and this time a tear got loose and trickled down her cheek. She was quick to wipe it away before it was noticed. "Girls, my girls," she looked at Bella first and then Blair. I need tight hugs to carry me through until the next time we are together, okay?" One by one, Bella and then Blair took turns hugging their mother's neck. Knox looked away when Skye closed her eyes to soak up those moments with them, and to say *I love you*. He had both girls in his arms when Skye waved to them. "Take good care of yourself, and we will see you very soon," Knox spoke to Skye on behalf of their daughters. His voice was strong but his eyes were misty and he had cleared his throat twice while he spoke those words that were supposed to send her good vibes or encourage her to fight harder.

When he reached the door, Afton had been waiting right outside. "Girls," she said, "let's go get a candy bar or something fun from the vending machine." Knox watched her attempt to take the lead with them. "Stay," she said to him. "I know there's more you probably needed to say, but not in front of the girls." He choked on a sob, and Afton could have come undone right then and there. He too was coming apart at the seams, and it broke her heart to witness him that way. She turned and walked away with the girls. She would hold Knox and comfort him later. He was in pain too, just like she was, at the mere thought of losing Skye.

Knox closed the door and turned back to Skye. She was sobbing uncontrollably now that the girls could no longer see or hear her. He took long, fast strides to get to her. He never hesitated to wrap her into his arms and embrace her as he never had before. And they both cried for everything they meant to each other, and for a bond like no other that they could very well lose.

Knox slowly pulled back when Skye began to regain her composure. "I want you to know something," he stated, and she noticed his red eyes and tear-stained face. He was still very close to her, on the edge of the bed. "No one can replace you, ever. Our girls need you, so you fight when this full-on war with your cells begins inside your body. Stay strong and fearless like you are teaching our girls to be." *Our girls.* Each time he said it, she loved him more. And it was probably time to tell him so.

"Knox, what we have between us, what we share could be perceived as weird or odd," he chuckled a little as she continued, "but it's the most special connection I've ever had with anyone else. I have my sister bond with Afton and Laney. I am and will forever be in love with Dylan. But I've never had a best friend before. You fill that role so perfectly. I don't know how else to describe how much you mean to me, other than that way, and to tell you that I love you, Knox," she paused, and then said it again, "I love you."

Tears were freefalling off his face now. There were no boundaries between the two of them, not since the moment they met. Their connection was profound, even when they downplayed or ignored it. And it was appropriate now to say how they felt, knowing that chance may never happen again. "I love you, too, Skye Gallant. Come back to us, okay? The girls need you so much, and so do I." She touched his face with both of her hands. She leaned forward to brush his disheveled hair away from his eyes and then she pressed her lips to his forehead. "I'll be fine. I promise. I don't want to bail out on my bestie." They both laughed through their tears and soon afterward Knox left to find the girls and Afton.

Chapter 23

Her sisters were the last to be with her before the medical team, including Dylan Fruend, would take over. The three of them sat in chairs, which formed a half circle near the window. Skye needed to get out of that bed for a little while.

She could sense the sadness, and she didn't want too many tears among them right now. Some, however, would be inevitable. "How do I thank you both for being here?"

"You don't," Laney told her and winked at her. "You're our baby sis." Afton then patted her knee, as if to wholeheartedly agree.

"I know I've said this before," Skye began, "but look at us now. Mom would be so proud. Remember how she used to say be careful who you give your heart to?" Both Laney and Afton nodded, certainly remembering.

Afton thought of Sam, who was the first man she had given her heart to — until he no longer deserved it. Knox would now have her heart for the rest of forever.

For Laney it was Brad who held her heart and always would. The thought of losing his love now terrified her.

Skye's sisters may have believed she was the only one who listened to their mother and waited to finally give her heart to Dylan Fruend. But that was wrong. Skye thought of her high school love. She was with Chris Hamilton for six months until he broke up with her. She thought she would die from that heartbreak then. It wasn't merely a crush, or puppy love. She wasn't just seventeen and only wanting to believe she had fallen in love. That was why, twenty years later, she seduced him. Because she knew she could. She was much more confident and sexier and more experienced with men. It wasn't just about the sex though and it wasn't the first time they had gotten together. She wanted, unbeknownst to him, to conceive a baby. Bella had her father's thick dark hair, and a few other striking features. Skye had no regrets.

It's not that she wanted to confide in her sisters with the secret she had kept, she only wondered if she should. She could be at the end of her life, and certain memories and thoughts had consumed her lately.

"Remember the game we used to play — tell me something I don't know?"

Both Afton and Laney shook their heads. "We can't bring that back!" Afton stated adamantly. "Some things are better off unmentioned."

"I remember that game being how I told you both that I had lost my virginity to Brad," Laney laughed out loud.

"Let's play it again, please?" Skye pressured them.

"Oh my gosh, no," Afton was adamant again.

"Oh what's the real harm, Aft? It's just us. We know our secrets are safe with each other." Laney, like Skye, wondered if she should share something with them that had been weighing her down.

"You go first then!" Afton stated, or practically demanded.

"Okay," Laney agreed, and then paused. "I'm drinking again." There was total silence in the room now. *Had her sisters felt disapproval or disappointment? Or perhaps, judgment?* She had confessed to something she kept so well hidden the past few months. To tell them was altogether different than to have Brad know she failed him. "Brad doesn't know."

"Oh Laney," Skye sighed.

"I know. What a pitiful mess I am." Laney couldn't look at either of her sisters right now, but she continued to speak. "I bargained with God. I told him if he saved Liam, I would never take another drink again. Well he saved him, and I broke my promise. The worst part of this for me is I don't even like alcohol anymore. I just have to have it."

"It takes courage to admit something like that," Afton praised her, and reached for her hand. "You will overcome this one day, I know you will."

"I'll bet neither one of you can top my secret," Laney laughed at herself, and truly believed that were true.

"This has been on my mind and maybe it's even the reason I started this personal, and potential to be risky, game tonight." Afton and Laney listened raptly. "Bella was conceived on purpose. Her biological father had no idea of my plan to get pregnant that night, and he doesn't know she exists. But I think you should both know, just in case." And that was all she implied about the possibility of dying from myeloma if this living cell trial failed, or thereafter. "It happened on the night of our 20th class reunion. I knew Chris Hamilton would be back in town. He lives in California now. He moved there for medical school right after high school, several months after he dumped me. He's a pediatrician now, and I had heard he was in the process of getting divorced. Then he showed up at the class reunion alone."

"So you seduced a former lover?" Laney asked her, in disbelief.

"Of course Bella is Chris Hamilton's blood. Look at that hair." Afton was lighthearted about this truth, and that surprised Skye a little.

Skye smiled. "I knew he had damn good genes. And I did love him once."

"Sneaky and smart," Laney noted.

"I don't ever want him to know about Bella, if you both understand what I'm saying. Please. But if there is ever a dire circumstance for Bella and I am not here, I will want you to guide her to him." It was understood that Skye was referring to an unforeseen health issue.

"What if Bella asks about him one day? I mean directly to you, because you are going to be around for it all," Afton spoke as a matter of fact.

"I hope she will be fulfilled having both Knox and Dylan as her fathers. But I will cross that bridge only if necessary. Or, the two of you must do it for me if I'm gone."

The reveals in that room were getting all too real for Afton. She was next, but would she tell them what they were expecting of her?

"Okay Aft," Skye spoke to her as if on cue. "Tell us something we don't know."

"Knox and I had sex on the hidden stairway in our house once. I lured him there with a romantic path of candles."

They all laughed out loud.

"Nice try," Laney told her, but we already know the two of you get it any which way you can, anywhere."

Afton grinned. That was true. And then her smiled faded. "I know what you both want me to say here. All I've ever told either of you was that I was involved in Sam's disappearance but the less you knew the better off you would be."

"I don't think we need protecting anymore. He's gone and everyone seems to have forgotten about him." Laney's words saddened Afton a little. No one wanted to be both gone and forgotten.

"It's not the two of you who I'm protecting. It's myself and someone else. We share a secret that we vowed to take to our graves. It's a loyalty I will not disrespect. I will play this game though and admit to you both that Sam is not missing, he's dead."

"And you know how it happened?" Skye asked.

"Yes," Afton answered.

"Did you kill him?" Laney prodded for more.

"No," Afton answered again. And it was the truth. Jess killed Sam to save Afton's life. It mirrored an act of self-defense. But they both were responsible for disposing of the body.

While Afton's sisters were relieved that she had not murdered her own husband, they still knew what had happened to him definitely was bad. And that Afton likely had a hand in his permanent disappearance.

"This is intense," Laney noted.

"It certainly got our minds off this potential goodbye among us." Skye needed to address that now.

"You're not going to die," Afton reacted, and she hoped with her entire being for that to be true.

Talk of the secrets revealed among them ceased. They were back to focusing on Skye.

She cried when, one by one, her sisters held her close and encouraged her to believe that the only end in sight was for the myeloma. She had a lot of living left to do.

The moment they were gone, the door opened again. Skye was still in mid sobs when she saw Dylan standing in the doorway. He wore powder blue scrubs, and in one hand at his side he carried that weathered and worn duffle bag.

She smiled through her tears. "What is this? A sleepover?"

"This is my way of showing you that I'm going to be here through it all. My trusty bag is packed for the extended stay."

She wouldn't want anyone else by her side for this drastic experiment with her life. Skye was both ready to begin and terrified of the outcome.

Chapter 24

Everyone else had gone about their lives while Skye was basically quarantined on the third floor of Regional Minneapolis. She was beyond grateful for Dylan to be with her around the clock.

The blood from her body ran through a dialysis-like machine with too many tubes extracted from it and then back into her. Skye swore she was drained of every last drop. Dylan reminded her that her blood was indeed circulating back into her body once the machine spun off the targeted cells. Those would be collected for immediate lab work. It took a total of eight hours before the necessary cells were retrieved and the rest of the blood components were returned to Skye's body. Skye was exhausted from the procedure, and Dylan encouraged her to rest. He then spent hours observing in the lab.

Samples of Skye's DNA and her own cancerous cells were joined in order to be re-engineered to recognize the cancer as the enemy. Once they were infused back into Skye's circulatory system, they were to kill all the cancer cells. Each dose of this living drug was unique and specific to the patient. It was genius, Dylan believed, as he watched the cell biologists at work. They were saving lives. Someone among them, or before them, had come up with a cure for myeloma. His confidence was beyond high for this to be a complete success for Skye. Within 24 hours, the engineered cells would be transferred back and reintroduced to Skye's body.

Skye would receive three doses of the live drug, divided into three increments of treatment every 24 hours. The wait period in between rounds was crucial to watch for the body's response in experiencing side effects or serious reactions to the live drug.

The first round of treatment went well. Dylan had tested Skye's light-chain numbers, which are indicators of cancer, and they had dropped from 6,000 to 4,500. Destruction was happening. The cancer was losing. He had informed her family the moment he read the results. They rejoiced with immediate responses to his text. Dylan didn't need to remind them that this was one of three treatments. They all knew, and everyone would continue to wait for more good news.

When Skye opened her eyes, Dylan was by her side. He wore a wide smile on his face as she tried to reciprocate one. She was too exhausted to move. She closed her eyes again. He wanted to tell her that her that it was working, the cancer was being destroyed in her body. But that would have to wait. Maybe she would be stronger after the next round of treatment. His research had shown that every patient was different. Some were sitting up and eating meals by now, where others had slept through a good portion of the 72 hours of triple infusions.

Twelve hours after the second infusion, things began to drastically change for Skye. Her body had a severe reaction when her natural immune system overwhelmingly responded to the therapy. Dylan had read about this happening before. There were so many cancer cells under attack that Skye's body was stunned by the immune response and she spiked a strong fever.

Dylan was by her side, but she hadn't been fully consciousness in two days. The medical staff was working around the clock, still, but this time it was to administer supportive therapy to counteract her body's strong reaction. Dylan met with the medical team's leader and was crushed when he was told her light-chain numbers, the actual indicators of the cancer left in Skye's body, had surged from 4,500 to over 6,000 again. They were back to where they started. Only worse — because of the fever. The cancer was winning the fight.

Skye's family was there. They were in the waiting room on the second floor of Regional Memorial, which was where Dylan instructed them to be. When he took the elevator down there to meet them, he found Afton and Knox, and Laney and Brad. They all bore worrisome looks. Their initial plan was to meet back there after all three of Skye's treatments were completed. There had only been two. One look at Dylan Fruend and they all knew they had every right to be sick with worry.

They all four stood up from their chairs against the wall in the waiting room the moment Dylan walked in. He looked drained. He needed to take a shower. He needed to change his scrubs. He cared about none of that though because they were losing Skye. And he alone was to blame.

He heard Afton first, and then Laney. And maybe Knox spit out a question in there too. It was all a blur. Brad was the only one silent and just waiting.

How is she?

What's happened?

Has something changed since your good news?

Dylan pulled off the surgical cap on his head and held it in both of his hands, like a towel in his grip that he was repetitively twisting and ringing out. "The second round of treatment wasn't as successful as the first," he began, and he watched both Afton and Laney reach for each other, as the men stood close behind them. "She spiked an intense, high fever that we have been battling to bring down and hopefully eventually break so she can receive the third round." It was crucial to give the patient all three rounds, Dylan knew that, but as of now Skye's body would not be able to handle another infusion. She would not survive. *And how in the hell was he supposed to tell her family that?*

"What are they saying up there? This medical team that you brought in, have they seen this happen before?" Knox was the first to want answers.

"It's happened before, yes. There are what we call light-chain numbers, remember my first text a couple days ago? Those numbers had started to go down after treatment number one. Those same numbers have now surged to indicate that there is more cancer in Skye's body than when we started."

"A reverse effect? Oh my God!" Laney reacted. "What does this mean? No more medical terms. Tell us in English, what is going on inside Skye's body right now?"

"The cancer is winning..." was all Dylan was able to say. He watched the four of them form an emotional huddle. They were holding each other up so no one would fall to their knees. They all had each other's backs. Their strength as a family was phenomenal. They all were pulling for Skye to survive. She had to have felt those vibes. And this time Dylan was the outcast. The only connection he had to all of them was Skye. They were counting on him to save her, and he was failing. She was a mother to those two baby girls for God's sake. Her life had to be spared.

Dylan spoke again. "I have to get back to her. I'm sorry to gather all of you like this, but—" he stopped talking. It was understood that this was not the kind of news he could share by text or phone call. He finally just began to walk away, and then he turned back. Afton had not spoken to him, or even looked at him. It was Knox and Laney who had addressed him. He looked at her now. She shot him a glance that confirmed what he already felt. He was to blame. He could have turned away and kept walking, but instead he spoke to only Afton. "I will never forgive myself if Skye does not pull through this. I guess I was that cocky son of a bitch after all. I was so sure I knew enough about immunology to understand that what they were trying to do had a very good chance of success." His words were directed only at Afton. She had lashed out at him with those very same words, and he had not given them a second thought. Until now.

Dylan heard a few of them speak up.

No. You're not to blame.

This isn't over yet.

Go. Be with her. We will be here.

None of those words of encouragement had come from Afton. And when Dylan made it to the doorway, his back was turned when he felt someone grab him by the shoulder which forced him to spin around. It was Afton. There were tears streaming down her face. She opened her arms to him, and both the doctor and the grown man in him instantly succumbed to feeling like a helpless child. He fell into her, and she held him while he openly cried for the woman he loved but was about to lose. Afton forced him to look at her. She was like a big sister, or even a nurturing mother. She was unraveling in her pain, but she had somehow found the strength to reach out to Dylan. "Save her. I know you can."

He nodded. She spoke again.

"But if we lose her... we will know that you did everything possible. You are a part of this family, Dylan Fruend. Always remember that." Dylan leaned into her and whispered *thank you* before he rushed back up to the third floor. He felt the renewed fight within him.

Chapter 25

Dylan sat by Skye's bedside reapplying a cold compress to her forehead. She remained mostly unconscious and continued to burn up, as one of the nurses had stated. They now were aware that the fever was stemming from serious anemia, as Skye had an extremely low red blood cell count. They needed a better plan of action. Dylan was going to step out and consult with the medical team in the lab. He would catch the nurse who walked in next. He didn't want to leave Skye for long, but he felt useless to her now as this cell war was raging inside her.

The door to Skye's room opened and a man in scrubs entered. Small framed. Twirly mustache. He stood up and rushed over to him. "Dr. Wright?"

"I had to come. I was informed that the treatment went haywire." It was an odd, old term to use, but Dylan instantly responded.

"She started off great, her numbers plummeted after the first round. But then, this reaction with the second round sent everything soaring. We can't bring down the fucking fever!" From one colleague to the next, Wesley understood Dylan's panic and anger.

"It appears that the cancer is winning," he stated, and Dylan wanted to scream at those words. *How could this be happening? This man, this survivor of the very same blood cancer, was standing in front of him completely cured and reaping the benefits of being alive. The very same was supposed to happen to Skye. She was stronger and healthier than most of the others who were fortunate to survive a live cell trial. All fairness had left the building, and Dylan was not only scared but he was desperate.*

"I am out of options to save her. I need something. Anything. I researched my brains out for months on end. I had every 'i' dotted and every 't' crossed. I tracked you down so I could look a cancer-cured-survivor in the eye to believe it could happen again to anyone, but especially for the woman I want to share the rest of my life with. What a fool I was to do this to her, and to her family."

Wesley Wright listened to the desperation in his voice. "I didn't come here to offer my sympathy for something gone wrong. We are going to intercept treatment." The first thing Dylan thought was her fever was too high to push this, but he didn't object as he listened for his explanation. "We are going to treat her with chemotherapy to eradicate the abnormalities and hopefully it will reach the myeloma. We need to make room for new cells immediately."

"And that has proven to work in a case gone wrong like this?" Dylan questioned him.

"*When* it works," Wesley Wright emphasized, "we will act fast with the third round." And that third round would determine Skye's fate.

"This is our only option isn't it?" This was an experiment with life or death that could instantly go either way. They truly were grasping at straws to contradict this war that the cancer clearly was winning.

"We cannot wait out this fever while she has cancer cells that are multiplying."

"Just help me save her," Dylan heard himself say, as he agreed to put Skye through another trial infusion.

∼

Two days later, a text from Dylan Fruend read, *All meet at Afton and Knox's house in one hour.*

Afton and Laney were in the kitchen with Knox. This was the part where Afton would have opened a bottle of something alcoholic to calm her nerves, and everyone else's but there was Laney and the fact that she was an alcoholic who was still sneaking fixes here and there. *So scratch that idea.*

Knox peeked into the living room to be sure the girls were still busy at play. Bella was overprotective of her baby sister, which always meant they played well alone. Laney sighed and looked at Afton. "I know I've said this, three hundred times since I walked in the door, but the last couple of days of no news have gotten my hopes up that the third round was working and Skye was improving. But Dylan's text scares me. Why is he coming here?" None of them wanted to assume that *it was all over in the worst way,* but they couldn't help it.

The doorbell rang and they all three jumped to their feet. Knox pulled open the door for Dylan and he stepped inside. He wore a Minnesota Twins hoodie overtop of those same scrubs.

His typically clean-shaven look was scruffy and even his smooth bald head was sprouting sporadic hairs. He looked weathered and worn as if his forty-something body had aged in merely days.

Again, they all talked at once.

"How is she?"

"Just tell us."

"We are sick with worry."

Dylan found his voice, but it was shaky. "I need to see the girls."

Knox's face fell. Dylan was there to find comfort in the two little people that Skye left behind in this world. They were the only part of her that Dylan and the rest of them had to hold onto. Knox didn't look at Afton. He couldn't. She would read the emotion on his face. *It was over. Skye was gone. Damn it to hell, life was terribly unfair.*

Knox, Afton and Laney all stood back, but they watched Dylan drop to his knees and make his way to the girls playing on the floor. They were happy to see him, and both instantly crawled onto his lap. He touched their hair and pulled their little bodies close.

"Where's mommy? Were you with her?" Bella always asked the right questions. She didn't waste time on unimportant kid stuff.

They watched Dylan nod his head. "I have been with your mommy for days. She didn't feel good, so I, um lots of people in the hospital, tried very hard to make her better." Tears were streaming down Afton and Laney's faces as they held onto each other. Knox formed tight fists inside the pockets of his dress pants. He was angry now. *Why had this happened? He would never understand this.*

"Is she better now? When can we see her?"

They heard Dylan clear his throat. "The two of you were the first I had to see. Your mommy would be here if she could be. Instead, she wanted me to tell you that she misses you both so much, but she's getting better. She's going to be healthy again very soon."

Afton, Laney and Knox looked at each other for reassurance, to be sure they had all heard right. Dylan turned his head around with a wide smile on his face. There were tears in his tired eyes when he said, "Skye wanted me to tell the girls first."

They rejoiced. They hugged. They were still crying, but this time those tears were ones of joy and gratitude.

Dylan immediately stood up from the floor. "This crisis is over. Her numbers indicating the cancer plummeted from 6,725 to 5. We tested twice. Skye's body finally sustained a complete response to the live drug. Cured is not too strong of a word to use at this point."

Afton grabbed him by the neck and the first thing she said was, "You saved her."

"No, it wasn't just me in there," Dylan begged to differ because he knew that medical team of cell biologists were pure geniuses led by Wesley Wright, who was hands-down a hero.

"Take the credit like a tried and true cocky son of a bitch," she kept her voice low and Dylan shook his head at her and grinned. That inside joke would now live on forever in their family.

Chapter 26

Laney eventually made her way home. She felt unbelievably happy. *Her sister was going to live!* She already shared the news with Brad and the boys when she called earlier. She walked into the kitchen to find Brad waiting for her. He was seated at the table and there was no sign of dinner having been cooked or eaten.

"Hey there," she smiled at him. "God it feels good to be home and to know that Skye is going to walk out of that hospital soon, healthy. Can you believe she's cured? The cancer is gone!"

"That's wonderful news," Brad was sincere, but not overjoyed. Before she could ask what was going on, he spoke again. "You should have a drink to celebrate, huh?"

"What?" she froze as she spoke.

"Oh you heard me. Run on upstairs and grab a bottle of wine under the sink. You know the leaky faucet that was dripping last night while we were trying to sleep? I fixed it today, but not before I moved all the stuff out from underneath the cabinet. How long have you been drinking behind my back?"

"It's not what you think."

"No? So that was just an old stash from before?" Brad was actually hopeful that were true.

"Not exactly but I—"

"Then how long, Lane?"

"It's a sip here and there, Brad. A few weeks ago, I caved, but it's different this time. You have to realize it is. I'm not drinking too much. I have not been drunk. It's just something I cannot totally cut off, but it's under control. Can you understand that?"

"I understand that it starts out that way. It's the same worn out repetitive pattern. A little bit becomes a little bit more. One glass becomes two, and eventually one bottle is emptied and you're needing more."

"I'll quit. I did it before, I'll do it again."

"Those are classic words from an addict."

"You're angry with me."

"More like disappointed."

He was going to tell her to leave again. She expected it, and the funny thing about it was Laney felt different about her drinking this time. She wanted to stop, but Brad never gave her the chance to explain that.

～

"Where's dad?" Liam asked Laney a few hours after Brad confronted her about drinking again and then walked out without another word. She had no idea where he went and she had not tried to reach him.

"Out," Laney said, sitting in the dark living room.

"Do you know where?"

"No."

"Was he mad?"

"Yes."

"He figured out that you are drinking again, didn't he?"

Laney stared at her son in the dark. She could see his face, and he could see on hers that she was surprised he knew.

"Don't think it wasn't obvious. And besides, once you're addicted to something, it's impossible to stop caving."

Laney looked at her son. He was too young to be that wise. He was her careless. reckless one. *Where was this coming from? Experience,* she realized.

"Is that your way of telling me that you are still vaping now and then?" Laney feared his answer. His lungs could not handle that.

"No, I'm not stupid. I know how damaged my lungs already are."

"Good," Laney told him. "I'm proud of you."

"Well I'm not feeling all that proud of my mother right now."

She closed her eyes to keep her calm and then opened them again. "I'm not too proud of myself either." She had disappointed Brad. And now her son too.

"Then do something about it before you lose Dad, and our family breaks up."

"I want to stop drinking," she told her son, "but when I finally do, it will not be for your father or for you and your brother. I tried that the first time. This time, it has to be for me. Just like how you stopped vaping because of your own set of lungs that you need to breathe with for the rest of your life, I'll do it for myself."

"I hope that you want to bad enough, mom. And I hope that you make up your mind to stop drinking before it's too late to fix what you've broken."

His words stung. Her son believed they were facing the ruins of a broken family because of her. And he was likely right. "Liam," she caught his attention before he left her alone in that dark room. "Remember the time we flew on an airplane to Disney World the summer before you and Luke started kindergarten?"

He nodded.

"Before we took off, the flight attendant told everyone to put the oxygen mask on yourself first before helping others around you. I realized something then. As a parent, I can only effectively manage my kids as well as I am feeling. Self-care is imperative for everyone. I seem to have lost sight of that."

Liam walked up the stairs now. And Laney had no idea that Brad was listening to every word of their conversation from the kitchen as they had not heard him come home.

~

One week later, Laney had taken a six-week leave of absence from teaching. She told her family what she was going to do. They could visit her on the weekends if they would like. It might give her the strength to carry out her hope to become a recovered alcoholic.

She drove herself to the Eden House in Minneapolis, which was an alcohol rehabilitation facility. She never asked Brad to bring her. They were still very distant with each other. He was obviously terribly hurt that she had lied to him. Truth be told though, Laney still felt like her husband did not fully understand her sometimes. She still believed that her drinking problem began when raising their boys, namely Liam, became challenging. She was the sole disciplinarian and it just became too much for her to battle Liam's defiance and Brad's inability to separate being a fun dad with a responsible father. He had his imperfections too. He just couldn't see the error of his ways. Their marriage wasn't perfect but their lasting love was worth every ounce of effort. Her first order of business was to get sober and to stay sober. Then, she hoped Brad would meet her halfway to save their marriage.

Laney sat in a large room with twenty-something folding chairs formed into a circle. Not all of them were occupied. She didn't look around. She kept to herself. She wasn't there to make friends or come to anyone else's aide. This was about her. Laney Potter was out for herself on this one.

The leader of this session called it to order. There wasn't much chatter or raucous to calm. Everyone seemed edgy or nervous. Probably because speaking in front of people wasn't for everyone, nor was it easy under these circumstances. *Hi, I'm Laney Potter and I'm a loser. Well, not really, but dependence on alcohol had brought her to her lowest point ever in her entire life.*

The first guy's name was Bob and he was soft spoken.

The second woman's name was Sharon and she didn't seem to mind that the attention was on her.

Third, it was Laney's turn already. *Shit. Why hadn't she sat further down in that circle? Was she ready for this? Yes. She. Was.*

"Hi. I'm Laney. And I have a drinking problem. I am an alcoholic."

She heard the crowd, people who were all just like her, respond in unison. "Hi Laney."

The person next to her did not have a chance to stand before another guy at the far end of their big circle stood up. Everyone instantly looked at him. Laney did, too. Her eyes widened and she felt her cheeks redden. *What the hell was he doing here?*

"Hi. I'm Brad. I don't have a drinking problem. Never have. But my wife does. I'm here because I want to go through every step of this program with her. You see, I've failed at understanding what she's been through. I'm learning that addiction isn't her fault. I want to understand this better, and her, so I can help her through it."

Tears were rolling down her cheeks. *Was something like this even allowed? She doubted so.* She didn't care though. She stood up and ran to him. He wrapped his arms around her, and she heard him say, "I'm so sorry."

Chapter 27

"Did you know that it takes ten years to declare a missing person dead?"

Afton looked at Jess from across the funeral home parlor. They were going out to dinner and the sooner they were out of that place the better Afton would feel. "You're not seriously bringing this up, are you?"

"Ten years from someone's disappearance, a motion to declare the person legally dead can be filed in court. After that, another ten years must pass before the person is actually declared legally dead."

"As Sam's widow, are you asking me to mark my calendar or something? Because if you are, you can think again. Why would I, why would we, possibly want to dredge up something that should be forgotten?"

"Have you ever thought about this?" Jess was in rare form, and Afton wanted no part of this discussion.

"No, but obviously you have."

"What about when you and Knox get married? Legally, you are still married to Sam."

"Sam is dead, which frees me in my mind and heart to marry Knox. What's on paper doesn't matter. We've already talked about having an unofficial ceremony for the books, but for us it will be the real thing, because it is. Sam is no longer my husband."

"You're right."

"But?"

"I think about death, which can't be helped because I'm a mortician in this industry, and I see how important it is to have a marker somewhere on this earth after you die. Even people who choose cremation question what that means for them not to have their name chiseled in stone with that dash between their birth and death dates. Some people don't give it a second thought, but I personally want that."

"Believe me, this world isn't going to forget Jess Robinson — at least the men won't." Afton teased and rolled her eyes.

"Hush. I've lived and learned." Jess was referring to her affair with Patrick Robertson. His death was ruled accidental, but Afton still wondered if he lost his mind over Jess and then took his own life.

"That's what you said after Sam..." Afton reminded her.

"I know it, but this time I am on the straight and narrow, I swear it."

"Why?"

"You heard that Saint Paul's Chief of Police retired right?"

"No! How did I miss that news?"

"Curt Weh wrapped up his career and we have a new chief."

"And who is that?"

"He's a fifty-something sexy-as-hell man in uniform."

"Jess, stay away from the law enforcement men, please. That's not a good idea for you."

"Listen, he's around my age, he's been divorced for a decade. I can actually have a drink in public with him because neither one of us is sneaking around."

"Have you?"

"Have I what?"

"Gone out with him?"

"Yes, twice. He asked me out after his great aunt's funeral that I handled here."

"That's creepy."

"Only to you."

"Maybe," Afton shrugged.

Jess smiled. "He's good for me. I'm happy getting to know a man the appropriate way. Planned dates. Good conversation. Intoxicating good night kisses."

"Do you talk in your sleep, Jess?"

"How should I know? And I haven't gone to bed with him yet, since you just implied that I have."

Afton shook her head and then started to giggle. "Just live your life. Do what you do. Of all the people in my life, I completely trust you the most. How ironic is that? I know it's because we went through something absolutely crazy and we've proven ourselves to each other like no one else. Our loyalty was tested and it's rock-solid."

Jess was close enough to Afton now to reach for her hand. She held it momentarily. "You haven't told anyone? Not Knox? Your sisters? Your children?"

"No. That's too many people, Jess."

"I know it."

"You'll always keep this secret too, right?"

Jess nodded her head. "Always."

Chapter 28

Dylan and Skye seized a weekend getaway to St. Louis. They saw a major league baseball game at Busch Stadium when the Minnesota Twins lost to the St. Louis Cardinals. They also had dinner on The Hill with Dr. Wesley Wright. Skye had known how that man came through when the clinical trial with the living drug had looked grim for her. She and Dylan would be forever grateful to him. He was a gracious, kind man who put others first. This weekend was going to be a special one for the couple, as Dylan had confided in his friend and colleague that he was going to propose to Skye. Wesley Wright wanted nothing to ruin their joy, and that was why he kept to himself that after five years his myeloma had returned. What he would do now to fight his battle remained to be seen.

~

They held hands and walked down Main Street in St. Charles, Missouri. It was a glimpse of past history on the cobblestone streets with original buildings that dated back to the birth of the State of Missouri. They reached the corner of Main Street and Dylan stopped walking. "This is beautiful. It's magical, almost like a step back in time," Skye told him as she stood with him and really had not even questioned why he stopped there.

"That's why I brought you here. I wanted to you get that feeling."

He smiled at her and turned toward the street corner where a carriage had just pulled up on cue. "Our ride is here."

"Are you serious? I've always wanted to take a carriage ride!" He knew that. Her sisters had told him when he asked for ideas to make Skye's dreams comes true. They also knew that he was going to propose to her on this trip.

"I'm serious. He helped her up, inside the carriage. There was a bottle of champagne on ice in there for them.

Skye was giddy, and so taken by this idea. She would catch herself looking around and then back at Dylan. The wide smile on her face was so permanent that her cheeks hurt. Dylan turned to her now. "My life hasn't been the same since you walked into my office."

"Oh my gosh, you're proposing to me, aren't you!"

He dropped his head and chuckled. "For once in your life, could you not speak what you are thinking the moment that it enters your mind?"

She pressed her lips together, to trap any other words that wanted to fly out. This was his moment to speak to her. And as she listened, Skye was bursting with love and happiness.

"I wanted to heal you," he began talking again, and this time his face grew serious. "It was almost as if I instantaneously knew your life was as important to me as my own. Whatever lies ahead, I want to be yours — heart, mind, body and soul. I love you, Skye Gallant. And yes, I'm asking you to be my wife...." He held up his hand and on the tip of his pinky finger was a very large halo diamond ring. Skye gasped. She watched him take it off his own pinky and slide it onto her finger. *And here she once thought taking a carriage ride would be a dream come true.*

Skye threw her arms around his neck and her lips were now inches from his. "Yes, I will be your wife!" She laughed through her tears when her lips met his like it was the first time their worlds collided in passion. When they parted, Skye had something else to say. "For so long, I didn't think I needed this kind of love in my life. I was self-sufficient and content alone, and then I had babies who changed my world. But it was you who showed me that nothing looks, tastes, or feels the same unless I'm sharing it with someone else… with you. Dylan Fruend, you saved my life —and me— in so many ways. I cannot even begin to convey the depth of my love for you."

"You don't have to," he reassured her. "I get it. I know it. And I feel it. I couldn't love you and your little girls more. The three of you complete me."

He earned himself another intense kiss and she quietly asked him when their carriage ride would be over.

He chuckled at her. "I thought this was your dream ride?"

"No, this journey with you is my dream ride."

Epilogue

Bella Gallant never knew her biological father. She wondered about him now and then, but she never set out on any crazy quest to find him and to reveal that she was the daughter he never knew existed. She was a senior in high school the first time she asked her mother about him. Skye reminded her daughter of the two fathers she had by her side lifelong, and then told her the partial truth. She had gotten pregnant on purpose, to conceive a child with a man she once loved. But, another year later, Skye was taken aback when her daughter had decided on a plan for her own future. She wanted to go to medical school and become a pediatrician. The power of DNA had dumbfounded Skye. Her reaction was so strong that she ended up revealing the truth to Bella. *Her birthfather was a pediatrician.*

Bella was now bookended by Knox and Dylan. For a girl who had lived the first couple of years of her life without a father, she definitely hit the jackpot with the two men who loved and raised her, each as their own. She was 29 years old now. She was a practicing pediatrician. And today, she was a stunning bride.

Her entire life, she had been surrounded by genuine, solid, intense love in her family. Her mother and Dylan. Afton and Knox, the man she chose as a toddler to call Daddy. Laney and Brad. All of those couples in love in Bella's life had shown her by example what it meant to ride out the storms together. Their lives were full of ups and downs, but who they loved and who loved them back was all that mattered at the end of the every day.

The wedding was held at Mears Park, twenty-five years after Afton and Knox fell in love there. It's where they shared their first kiss on that bench near the walking trail. The three sisters agreed that absolutely everything was special about Bella's day. They sat together under a white party tent now. Their feet hurt in heels that weren't nearly as high as they once could wear, and they joked about that when they clinked their wine glasses together. Laney was sipping sparkling water. She had been sober for more than two decades. And every routine blood test for Skye continued to be cancer-free. The Gallant girls were healthy and happy, only getting older.

"We are all very fortunate to see this day, especially me," Skye spoke from a grateful heart. "Bella was telling me earlier that we have all taught her something about love. Afton — you are the selfless lover. Our family knows all too well that Blair Manning would not be here if it weren't for your noble, self-sacrificing act for the man you love. Afton dabbed her eyes. *She still hated to cry!* Laney — you are the fierce lover. No matter what, you don't give up or give in."

"And what kind of lover are you?" Afton asked her youngest sister.

"She said I was a brave lover," Skye choked on her words, "because I brought her into the world with the intent to raise her as a single mother. And then there was the miracle of Blair. I was sick. I wanted a sibling for my daughter. You two know the story. And lastly, there's Dylan. I fought death to be with him."

Several decades of living had been shared among the Gallant girls. Father time may have touched all of their bodies as their physical appearances had inevitably changed. But their souls remained — selfless, fierce, and brave.

~

Afton had never forgotten what Jess told her. *It meant something to have your name chiseled in stone with that dash between your own birth and death dates. It was proof that you existed and mattered.* Twenty-five years after Sam Drury went missing, he was declared legally dead.

There was a modest tombstone in Saint Paul's Catholic Cemetery set above empty ground. Afton and Jess made their way, arm and arm, through tall grass and uneven soil. It was the first time they both had been there to see it. As his widow, Afton saw to it that it was done. There was a marker for Sam Drury's life. It was simple. She wasn't about to chisel in stone that he was an amazing husband and doting father. He once was, she supposed. But those days were long forgotten in her memory. Her life after 50 had most definitely been the better half.

"What changed your mind about doing this for him?" Jess asked as they stood over Sam's tombstone.

"I've mellowed through the years," Afton teased, as Jess laughed under her breath.

"It's strange to think there is nothing beneath our feet. No coffin, no remains at all." Jess noted.

"Right," Afton agreed. "We could go to the landfill if you want a chance to be near what's left of Sam Drury." It was inappropriate, but funny, and they both laughed out loud as they recalled putting his cremated remains into a trash bag and setting it on the curb for trash pickup day in Saint Paul.

"Should we say something about him, or pray?" Jess asked Afton.

"I've thanked God enough for changing my life after this man was gone. I'll pass on the prayer for Sam." Afton was serious this time. "But if you want to say something, how about if we take turns noting what we remember most about him?"

"Sure, okay." Jess appeared to think that was a good idea. A special way to honor Sam's memory. There had been some wonderful times with him. It was just difficult to remember him as a good person.

"I'll go first since I slept with him first." They both cackled. Good thing they were alone out there in the cemetery. "He liked to dip his dry toast in his coffee every single morning."

"That's it? That's all you have?" Jess' mouth hung wide open. This obviously wasn't going to be a sentimental remembrance of a man they both shared great portions of their lives with.

"Yep." Afton shrugged. "Try to top that if you can."

Jess never missed a beat. "He was smoking hot right up until the very end."

They hooked arms amid their loud laughter, and turned and walked away. That was the first and last time they paid respects to Sam Drury's memory.

About the Author

It's bittersweet to say goodbye to a world of characters that I've spent so much time in since the release of this trilogy! It was gratifying to complete this story that I never intended to write in 3 parts, but it just inevitably happened when the lives of all these characters began to unfold. The Gallant sisters are intricate and unpredictable women that led me through a story that even I didn't know how it was going to end. With that said, from beginning, middle, to the end — I do hope you enjoyed the Stronger than Truth Trilogy.

I believe that some things are stronger than the truth. The friendship between Afton and Jess proved that theory to be most true. They were not close friends in Book 1 (Shared Silence). There was a lie between them. Jess betrayed Afton for an entire decade as she carried on an affair with Afton's husband, Sam. Those two women were the least likely candidates to ever become friends, much less likely — best friends. The self-defense murder coverup led the two of them through a test of loyalty which they survived, and they most definitely grew stronger and much closer throughout Book 2 (As We Are) and Book 3 (For Reasons Unknown). This is fiction, so anything will or will not happen. I would also like to think that my readers did not want to see Afton and Jess get caught, nor have to pay for any crimes.

With the release of my 23rd book, I continue to be grateful for the opportunity to entertain all of you — my loyal readers. This would not be possible without you!

As always, thank you for reading!

love,

Lori Bell

Made in the USA
Middletown, DE
07 November 2019